MILLIONAIRE BEST FRIEND

NATASHA L. BLACK

MAYA

I reached into the bag of flour in front of me and grabbed another handful. Sprinkling it across the table, I plopped the mound of what I hoped would eventually become a pie crust down in the middle of it. A poof of flour rose up in the air, and I tilted back to prevent it from getting all over me.

I glanced over into the kitchen to look at the clock on the oven. Marshall would be home in about two hours. This gave me just enough time to finish up my battle with the pie crust, fill it, and get it in the oven.

With any luck, it would just be ready to slide out golden, brown, and impressive when he walked through the door. I already had a clean, fresh apron waiting to be put on so that my appearance might look effortless instead of appearing well-greased and ready for seasoning.

The whole effect was supposed to be cute. We had just moved in together a few weeks before, and I was trying to seem domestic. I wanted Marshall to come home, and see me holding a freshly baked pie. Surely, he wouldn't be able to resist me. I had a whole scenario going on in my head, and if I could just get this crust to work out for me, it would be perfect.

I had certainly never been the sweet and demure housewife type. And that is exactly was what was supposed to make it so funny. Marshall and I moving in together with a huge step. I had never lived with another guy before. We had been together for three years, and people were always asking us when we were going to settle down and get married.

At twenty-three years old, I wasn't exactly inching toward my expiration date. In fact, I had never even seriously thought about marriage. Marshall and I were just living our lives, seeing where it took us. Moving in together was a sign that things were actually serious, and we had a future together.

It was a little scary when he asked me. I was used to taking care of myself, and the idea of sharing everything with him all the time was a bit intimidating. I wasn't sure how it was going to feel to depend on him as much as myself. Especially considering he pointed out his apartment was bigger, so I should move into his place instead of him into mine.

But the prospect of a new adventure was exciting, so I decided to jump straight in. Over the last few weeks, I had been doing my best to settle in and make it my home, too. I was looking forward to him coming home and sampling my pie. Maybe he would get the dirty little joke.

Finally, the crust started cooperating, and I was able to roll it out and transfer it into a pan. I grabbed a can of cherry pie filling.

I put the pie into the oven and went into the bedroom to try to clean myself up. I hadn't even gotten a chance to put my fresh apron on when I heard the front door open.

Looking over the clock, I saw it was a whole hour before Marshall was supposed to come home. I scurried out into the kitchen and found him staring at the dining room table still covered with a couple of inches of flour and wayward pieces of dough stuck to the wood.

"I'll clean that up," I said. "Don't worry about it."

"What happened in here?" he asked.

"It was supposed to be a surprise, but since you decided to come home early, I'll have to tell you. I baked you a cherry pie. Homemade crust and everything. Why are you home early?" I went up to him and looped my arms around his neck. "Not that I'm complaining."

I rose up on the balls of my feet to give him a kiss, but Marshall took hold of my wrist and stepped back slightly from me.

"Maya, we need to talk."

I laughed. "Don't worry about the table. It looks like a much bigger mess than it actually is. Plus, the pie is going to be worth it." I gave him a cheeky look. "The dessert will probably be delicious, too."

He didn't even crack a smile. "Maya, really. Come sit down." He moved my arms away from his neck and rested them down by my sides.

The humor drained out of me, and my heart started pounding a little. "Is something wrong?"

He didn't answer, but walked into the living room. I followed him and sat on the couch. He sat at the other end, purposely putting the entire middle cushion between us.

"Maya, there's no easy way to say this, so I'm just going to say it. It's over," he said.

And that was it. No explanation. No lead-up. Not even a half-assed attempt to let me down easy by using a bunch of euphemisms and flowery language. He didn't even tell me it was him and not me, or that he was setting me free to fly. Just that it was over.

And now I was really glad I used canned cherry pie filling.

I stared at him in utter disbelief. "What do you mean, it's over? I just moved in with you."

He looked down at his hands, drumming his fingers together, then straightening and flexing them like he had never seen them before. I couldn't understand what he was saying. We had been together for three years. I wasn't just a one-night stand who was getting too clingy and he wanted to oust from his house. It wasn't even a flash-in-the-pan relationship that got too serious, too quick.

This was three years of our lives. To a lot of people, we'd moved slowly. Several of our friends had met, dated, gotten engaged, and gotten married during the time of our relationship. One pair was even raising their first child. We were just getting to the moving-in stage, and I thought things were going really well between us. But suddenly, Marshall was pulling the plug without any explanation.

"I know," he said.

Suddenly the man who loved to hear himself speak and could babble on for hours about whatever topic randomly sparked his interest was the quintessential man of few words.

"How could you do this to me?" I asked. "We've been together for three years. You asked me to move in with you. You insisted I move into your apartment with you. I gave up my place so I could come live here. I work for your father. What am I supposed to do?"

He kept staring at his fingers. "I'm going to go somewhere else tonight, and I'll stay out of the apartment for the day tomorrow so you can get your stuff together."

And then he was gone. Not another word. He just got right up and walked out of the apartment. I sat there on the couch for a while, half expecting him to come back in and tell me it was some sort of really bad joke. Only it didn't make any damn sense, and he wasn't exactly the joking kind.

He left me sitting there confused as hell, barely even knowing what I was supposed to do next. I didn't know how long I had been sitting there, but the smell of burning pie crust was what finally snapped me out of my daze and got me up off the couch.

A couple minutes later, I stood in the kitchen holding the blackened pie, staring down at the crust I had worked so hard to make. If I was a more sentimental and poetic person, I would probably find some sort of parallel between the ruined pie and our relationship.

I tossed the pie into the trash and went into the bedroom. Something occurred to me the second I walked in and I headed for Marshall's dresser. Opening it, I found each of the drawers partially empty, like articles of clothing had gradually migrated out and ended up somewhere else. I didn't even notice before.

Slamming the drawer closed, I stripped down, changed into pajamas, and toppled into bed. The next morning, I was just as confused as I was when he walked out. Maybe even more. Part of me still thought he would come back. Maybe he would show up in the middle of the night and say he'd had a momentary freak-out, but came to his senses and everything was fine.

Yet when morning came, the apartment was still empty and quiet.

It was really over. At some point, I didn't even notice. Marshall had jumped off the relationship train and just left me to careen into disaster all by myself. Forcing myself to swallow it all down and look at the situation with stoic logic, I took a shower and started packing. I stuffed my clothes, toiletries, books, and kitchen stuff into my luggage. I stuffed whatever I could find that I thought might be mine into any boxes and bags around and tossed it into the bed of the pickup truck my dad left me when he died.

I should have just gotten in the truck and driven away right then. I was still feeling pretty calm and might have managed to get out of the whole debacle without falling apart. But instead, I decided I needed to go back inside. Though it had only been my home for a few weeks, it was where Marshall and I had spent a considerable amount of our time together for the last three years.

Seeing it stripped of the reminders of me hit me hard. I stood there in the middle of the living room, reminiscing about where my pictures and trinkets used to be displayed fondly, remembering that I had cleared out a section of shelves to put my books when I moved in. I felt so alone. Tears stung the backs of my eyes. I wanted to just stand there and cry. But I wasn't going to. Not right then, at least.

I deserved more than just a one-sentence breakup. After everything we had gone through together, Marshall needed to find the courage and tell me why he'd ended things with me. Even though I had a pretty good idea of it, considering the great exodus of his clothes. I needed and deserved that closure.

I left the apartment for the last time and got in the truck, heading right for the cabinet warehouse. It used to be wonderful that Marshall and I worked together at his father's company. It meant we got to see each other during the day and eat lunch together. For most of our relationship, we worked the same shifts and could even ride in together.

When our shifts changed a month ago and we no longer lined up, I didn't think anything of it. Now I couldn't help but wonder about that as well. I knew that was where he would be. He wouldn't be able to avoid me, so I could confront him there and get the answers I needed.

My stomach sank when I got to the warehouse and the receptionist told me Marshall was in his father's office. He never went in his father's office. In fact, most of the time he did whatever he could to not associate with his father during work. He always said he didn't want to look like he only got anywhere because of his dad.

I walked into the office and quickly discovered Marshall's sharp and to-the-point breakup technique was inherited. His father's firing technique was pretty much the same.

2

GREG

I t felt so good to be back at the compound. And I wasn't just glad to be here to support Darren. I missed every-thing about the environment, too. I was going to go crazy if I had to stay away from the track any longer. I had spent the last several months recovering from a nasty broken leg, and focusing on recovery had pretty much had taken up the majority of my time.

This accident had been the most terrifying moment of my life. As a racer, I knew it was a possibility that inevitably occupied the back of my mind. Nobody goes out onto a track believing they are invincible. If you choose to climb onto the back of a motorcycle and go in ovals at top speeds, you never think you are completely safe.

There were always risks. There was always the chance something could go wrong. All we could do was make sure our bikes were in the best condition possible, and train as hard as we could. I had done all of that. I worked my ass off on the track, trying to get the best I could.

It was a huge deal when the Freeman family asked me to race for their team. This was a dream of any rider in

Charlotte. The Freeman family was legendary. Even more so since the oldest son, Quentin, had taken over for his father. They were already well-known, but with Quentin's dedication and the impressive skill of the youngest brother, Darren, the company's success had skyrocketed.

And they wanted me to race with them. From the beginning, I, myself, am a man who has been satisfied with just to working on their bikes. Just having the opportunity to be around them and a small part of the success of the team was already a dream come true. Then came the fateful day when Darren asked if I rode.

It sounded so dramatic when I put it that way, but it was the truth. Darren and I were good friends by that point, and it was still an honor for him to ask me to show him what I could do. I never imagined he would be so impressed by me that he would suggest I start training to race. He went to bat for me with the family, and before I knew it, I was out on the practice track every day, polishing my skills.

The day I debuted in an actual race was one of the greatest of my life. Possibly *the* greatest. The rush was unlike anything I'd ever experienced, even better than I could have imagined. I didn't win, but I didn't care. I didn't expect to. Ranking in the top five was a huge accomplishment. It gave me a taste of what it felt like to overcome all those other men and sail over the finish line with them behind me. It made me want more. So, I worked harder. I trained more. I pushed farther. I got better, ranked higher.

But then I got cocky. Anger and arrogance were bad combinations when you're clinging to a chunk of metal going more than one hundred miles an hour surrounded by other people doing the same. It was especially bad when you added in hunger for power and success.

I wasn't the one who caused the wreck, but my own

arrogance didn't help it. Another rider clipped me, and I spiraled out of control. I skidded across the track my bike landed on me, dragging me. By all accounts, I shouldn't have made it off the track alive. When I did, it was the Freeman family who was there for me.

I woke up, and Darren was there by my bedside. Quentin barely left my side until the day I was discharged, and my mother came to take care of me while I recovered. I felt horrible for not being able to race and apologized over and over. I promised to find someone else to ride in my place so they wouldn't be in as much of a lurch.

There wasn't a single moment when they made me feel guilty. Not a single moment they were anything but supportive. They refused my offer and told me to think of nothing but getting better. They sent food, called constantly, and came to pick me up to bring me to the compound for visits when my mother was busy. They even came up with ways I could work and attend the races even if I couldn't ride.

They always said they considered me like family, but that was when I really felt it.

All I could think about was getting better and getting back out there on the track. Last week, it finally happened, and I'd spent every single second I could riding ever since then. That was what I was doing that afternoon. Most of the others weren't there, so I had the track to myself. When I heard tires approaching, I thought maybe Darren had come back for a bit of a friendly race.

I had just pulled into my slot at the garage, but would have been happy to head back out even after hours of riding already. When I turned around to greet him, I saw it wasn't him. The truck I did see pulling up down the access road shocked me.

I knew that truck, but I hadn't seen it in years. The same could be said for the girl in the front seat. Seeing her was both shocking and confusing. It had been so long, and I couldn't imagine what would have brought her here. Five years had passed since I had left my hometown and came here to Charlotte. And in those five years, I hadn't even spoken to Maya, much less seen her.

But there she was. I waited for her to hop out, but she didn't. The door opened slowly, and she climbed out almost like she was sliding from the seat. Like her body didn't have enough strength to hold her up. As soon as I saw her, I noticed how much she had changed. The five years had altered her, but there was one thing that stayed the same.

She was still impossibly gorgeous. At that moment, she looked like she had seen better days, but she was still incredible. Her hair was a bit longer. Her face was a bit thinner. Her eyes were red from crying, but she was still beautiful.

I rushed toward her.

"Maya! What the hell?" I pulled her into my arms for a hug. She clung to me, shaking.

There was definitely something seriously wrong. I couldn't remember a time I had ever seen her this upset. I held her there until she stepped back away from me. She looked into my eyes.

"I didn't know where else to go."

She managed to get the words out before the tears welling up in her eyes tumbled out and fell down her cheeks. Her shoulders shook, and it looked like her legs were going to collapse from beneath her. I looked down and saw her hand wrapped so tightly around her car keys that they were cutting into her skin.

Grabbing her up into my arms again, I held her tight against me and reached down to pry the keys out of her hand. She resisted, but finally I managed to wrench them free. Her arms clenched around me, and she held on like she was trying to find enough strength to keep on her feet.

I stood there with her for a few more moments, then started toward the building. She was still hanging on to me, so I had to grip her and maneuver her along with me as I headed for the breakroom. When I got inside, I brought her over to the couch and sat her down.

Along with a cup of coffee, I got a chunk of the coffee cake Minnie Freeman had baked that morning and brought them over to her. Maya took the cup and plate. She took a sip of the coffee and let out a trembling breath. I sat down close beside her and reached around to rub her back.

"What's going on?" I asked.

"I'm sorry to have come out here like this," she said.

"Don't apologize," I said. "You have nothing to be sorry for. Now, tell me what's going on."

"My life is falling apart," she said. She leaned forward and set the coffee and plate down on the table in front of her, then covered her face with her hands.

"Tell me everything," I said.

She drew in a breath and looked at me.

"I was with Marshall for three years. Everything seemed like it was going really well. Or, at least there wasn't anything wrong. You know what I mean? Like, we didn't fight all the time or have anything that was specifically going bad about our relationship. Everything was just..."

"Normal?"

"Yeah," she said. "Everything was normal. We had a good rhythm. We worked in the same place. His father's business, as a matter of fact. Then, we decided to move in together."

"Alright," I said, not sure where she was going with all this.

"He just unceremoniously dumped me, kicked me out of the apartment, and cost me my job, less than a month after I agreed to get rid of my own place and move in with him," Maya said.

Another wave of tears hit her so hard that her face dropped back down into her hands. She shook her head back and forth like she couldn't even believe she was telling me all this. Or maybe she couldn't believe that it was happening at all.

"Did he give you any explanation at all?" I asked.

"Nothing," she said. "I was at home, baking him a freaking pie. A pie. Can you even believe that? I even made the damn crust myself. I was going through all that to show him that I thought we were in a good place and our relationship was going well. He came home and said it was over. Just like that. It's over. Then he said he would leave so I could get my stuff. The next day, I went up to where we worked to talk to him and ended up finding out I didn't have a job anymore either. I don't have anything anymore."

My hands clenched tight at my sides, and the urge to go after the guy made the center of my chest ache. I knew nothing would come of me going back to my hometown. So, I just held Maya tight.

"Yes, you do," I said. "You have me. I've got you. You're fine now."

3

MAYA

It wasn't a shining moment in my life. I wanted it to think of it as showing humility and being willing to be vulnerable in this difficult moment. Instead, I just felt pathetic as hell. My entire life was falling down around me, the life I had once been so proud of and confident in. In fact, in all honesty, I had been nothing short of smug about it.

After all, I thought I had made it. Despite everything people told me when I was growing up, I got through high school. I even went to college. While I was there, I started dating Marshall, and it was like the whole world opened up to me. I already knew him. At least, I knew of him. He had gone to school with me when I was younger, but we hadn't run in the same circles.

The truth was, the one thing I knew about him was that he associated with people not known for being the most pleasant. Greg knew him better than I did. I remembered some of the things he said about him when we were younger and was hesitant when I ran into Marshall again.

But he didn't seem like what Greg said about him. He

was sweet and attentive then. People changed, I told myself. People grew up and didn't act like they did when they were teenagers. I'd decided to give him the benefit of the doubt and form my own thoughts about him.

After all, Greg wasn't around anymore. He had already left for Charlotte, and I hadn't heard from him in nearly two years by the time Marshall and I got together.

I might not have had too much domesticity in me, but that didn't mean I didn't eventually want to settle down. I didn't want to spend the rest of my life alone. And I definitely didn't want to do exactly what all the old ladies whispered about in the salon while they got their hair done. That was the birthplace of the grapevine and where reputations could be made and destroyed.

For me, the women already had my potential for a future dead in the water. According to them, the family I came from meant I would never amount to anything. I was doomed to nothingness before I was even born. They never even gave me a chance.

But I showed them. At least, that's what I thought. Getting an education and finding Marshall was far more than any of them ever expected for me. I wasn't going to jump right on the bandwagon and get married instantly, but I could build a life. I had a home and opportunities.

Then it all crumbled at my feet. I didn't even get a chance to prepare, to piece something together that would catch me. I just fell flat on my face. And this was where I ended up. Back where I always used to all those years ago. Right into Greg's arms.

He'd been my best friend for years. We'd seen each other through everything, and he was the one person I felt like never judged me. He always thought there was something more in me. But he ended up being the one who got out of our little hometown and started to make something out of himself and we'd lost touch. We hadn't seen each other in five years. There was a time when I thought I would never see him again.

After everything that happened, he was the only thing I could think of to go to. With nothing else left, I went to him. As pathetic and embarrassed as I was to be there spilling everything out to him, I was also relieved. I drove away from the cabinet warehouse, got on the highway, and didn't look back. I knew right then I couldn't stay in that town.

I didn't have a plan when I started driving. All I knew was there was nothing left for me back home, and I had to think of something else. It wasn't until a couple of hours later that I thought of Greg. Before he left, he told me he would always be there for me. I thought I could count on him, and now I was glad to know I wasn't wrong. He didn't even hesitate to tell me I could stay with him. There wasn't a second of doubt.

Once that was settled, Greg picked up my coffee and the chunk of coffee cake he brought me and handed them back to me.

"Eat," he said. "If I know you, you haven't even thought about eating or sleeping since all this happened. You need to take care of yourself."

I didn't argue with him. I took another sip of coffee and a bite of the cake. It was delicious, heavy on the cinnamon, just like I liked. When I finished eating, we went back out to the garage.

"This is my bike," he said, gesturing toward the impressive machine he was parking when I drove up to the building.

"And you really race this thing?" I asked.

"Well, I haven't been recently. I was in a pretty bad

accident a few months back, and I'm just now getting back on my feet. And on my bike. But I'll be back in action this season."

"Maybe I'll get to come see you ride," I said.

He smiled at me. "I hope so."

A few minutes later, two other men came walking up to the garage. Greg waved at them.

"Hey," he said. "I thought you weren't coming in today."

"Changed our minds," the older man said.

Greg laughed. "Just can't keep you away from here."

"He's not doing great at retiring," the younger man said. "I think he's actually here more now than he was when he actually worked here."

"Well, everything else is here. My wife's here. Three of my four sons. An honorary son. Two of my daughters-in-law. A couple of my grandchildren most of the time. Why would I wander around in an empty house when I could be here?"

I didn't even know who these people were, but I couldn't help but smile. Greg noticed and came over to put his arm around my shoulders.

"This is Maya. She's been my best friend for as long as I can remember. Maya, this is my teammate Darren Freeman, and his dad, Gus. As you just heard, Gus is technically retired, but he still spends a lot of time here."

"I'm not all the way retired," Gus said. "I still do the custom bikes."

"When Kelly isn't doing them," Darren said.

They all went right back into their conversation, seamlessly including me. I felt completely welcomed. None of them questioned why I was there. They were perfectly comfortable with me being on the racing compound and a part of whatever they were doing.

For the rest of the day, I hung out with them there at the garage. I watched as they worked on Greg's bike, making modifications and improvements, and talking to him about his practice runs that day. When the day was finally over and it was time to head out, I felt immeasurably better. I followed him home, hopeful that I'd made the right decision. This could be my fresh start.

Or at least, give me somewhere to hide out until I found that fresh start.

I followed Greg to a nice apartment complex. As soon as he put a code into a keypad at the gate, the doors split open. We drove through, and I noticed a large clubhouse with a sparkling pool behind it. A few moments later, we drove past a beautiful park. It was still light enough for children to be out playing on the massive playground, and couples wandered the walkways and sat underneath the trees.

Greg finally parked in front of a building toward the back of the complex and came around to the back of the truck. He reached inside and grabbed a box and a couple of bags out of the bed. He was all in, already helping me move in. He wasn't just expecting me to be there for the night and then find somewhere else the next day. It made my heart feel warm, but also brought back a little bit of that helpless feeling as well.

I grabbed a few things myself, but it would take at least one more trip to get everything inside. He led me in, and I looked around. It was a nicely sized apartment, neat, but somewhat sparse. Pretty much what I would expect a single guy like Greg to have.

"This is the living room," he said. "The kitchen is out there. Dining room over there. There's a little laundry room in the hall next to the bathroom. My bedroom is at the end of the hall. I have a second bedroom, but it doesn't have a bed in it. It has a couch, though."

"That's perfectly fine with me," I said. "I have no issues sleeping on the couch."

"No, no. We can get you a bed," he said.

"I'm already crashing your apartment with no notice," I said. "You don't need to worry about transforming a room for me. The couch is not a problem."

"Are you hungry?" he asked. "You barely ate anything at lunch."

Gus had ordered in from a little diner down the street. The boxed lunches looked delicious, and the few bites I took were wonderful, but I hadn't been able to build up much of an appetite. Everything that happened was still turning around in my stomach, making me feel uneasy. But now that I was here with Greg and felt a little more settled, some of my appetite was back.

We went into the kitchen, and he threw together a quick dinner of pasta and a side salad. We sat down and ate in comfortable near silence, something Greg has always provided me with instead of pushing an interrogation. Other people might have sat down and immediately started peppering me with questions, but not him. He was the type to give me the time I needed. If I wanted to tell him more, he would listen. If not, that was fine, too.

This was the way things had always been between us. He accepted me without hesitation.

It wasn't too long after dinner when I started feeling completely worn-out. It was like the adrenaline from the last two days had drained out of me, and I was left exhausted. After a quick shower, I went into the spare room. He had set up the couch with fresh sheets and pillows. A blanket was folded at the end. I changed into my pajamas and tucked myself in, falling asleep within seconds.

The next morning, I got up before Greg and went to make breakfast. It was the least I could do. He came in with a smile and grabbed a cup as it finished brewing.

"I'm going to call my landlord today and ask him about adding you to the lease. I want you to feel like you are really home here," he said.

It was enough to get the tears started again. I had so much on my mind and was so emotionally raw. I didn't want to feel it right then. I didn't want to focus on anything. So, I decided to turn my attention completely on Greg. Brushing the tears away, I really looked at him.

The last five years had changed him. I knew they had changed me, but somehow, I hadn't expected the difference in him. It was like he was frozen in my mind; kept exactly the way he was the night I said goodbye to him.

When he left our hometown, his tall body was gangly and young. Now he had filled out and looked grown and muscular. I had always loved his hair long. It just looked like him, but his new short hairstyle was good on him, too. Even though I was sad about my life in general, I wasn't blind.

I would have to have totally lost my mind to not notice how hot Greg had gotten.

4

GREG

When I went to bed that night, I couldn't fall asleep. I woke up that morning right there in that same bed and had no idea that day would be any different than any other. Just like every other morning, I got up, took a shower, and headed to the compound, thinking about nothing but my bike and getting out on the track.

But now I was back in that bed, and everything was different. My apartment wasn't empty. It wasn't just me anymore. All of a sudden, Maya was back in my life. Not only back in my life, but actually in my apartment. In the spare room that was supposed to be a second bedroom, but that I had never had reason to use that way. Even when my mother came to take care of me, she slept in my bedroom while I stayed in a hospital bed rented by the Freemans for me.

Not only could I not believe she was back in my life, but I was struggling to keep my emotions in check after everything she'd told me. As soon as she mentioned Marshall, I knew who she was talking about. She tried to just gloss over it when she was talking about her ex-boyfriend. She didn't want to get into the conversation with me about who he was.

She knew exactly what I thought of him. There was no ambiguity, no question about how I felt about Marshall or the idea of the two of them being together. It was hard to imagine that she spent three years of her life with that prick. I would have had a hard time believing she would have willingly spent three hours of her life with him.

Even back in school, I couldn't stand Marshall Brinkley. He was an entitled, rude, spoiled jackass who reveled in treating other people like shit. Especially the people he thought were below him, which were most people. Marshall came from the Brinkley family, one of the most well-to-do families in Shelby.

Not that they were anywhere near as affluent as the Freemans, but for Shelby, they were at the top of the food chain. And Marshall knew it. He didn't just take having money as a privilege or a blessing. To him, it was a sign from the universe that he was above everyone else.

I had to imagine he wasn't like that when Maya got with him. They hadn't known each other well in school. She didn't realize it, but I had put effort into keeping her away from him. Right around our junior year, he started making noises about being attracted to her, but I knew he would hurt her if he got a chance. So, I made sure to stay between them until he got bored and lost interest.

Apparently, that didn't last for long. They met up again sometime after I left Shelby, and he managed to weasel his way into a three-year relationship with her. Despite my efforts to keep her safe, he still got away with breaking her heart. I was angry for Maya. She deserved the world.

So, as I lay there in bed, thinking about her sleeping on the couch in my spare room, I tried to stop myself from getting up and going back to Shelby to punch Marshall right in his smug face. It might not have done a lot of good in fixing the situation, but it sure would have felt good in that moment.

It took a long time for me to finally will myself to sleep. When I woke up the next morning, my apartment smelled like fresh coffee and bacon. And I found Maya in the kitchen, making us breakfast. She always teased about not being good at the domestic stuff, and I would be the first to admit she couldn't bake to save her life. She once tried to make me cupcakes for my birthday, and they ended up like doorstops.

Now she was standing in my kitchen cooking up eggs, bacon, and pancakes. She couldn't bake to save her life, but she had always been a good cook. It was nice to see all that homemade food getting piled up onto platters and plates to be put on the table. I was used to starting my day going through a drive-thru for breakfast and hoping Minnie would have something waiting in the kitchen at the compound.

Maya seemed to be in better spirits and feeling a bit stronger until I mentioned I would get in touch with my landlord and ask about him adding her onto the lease. Of course that's when the tears dripped down her cheeks again. I didn't mean to make her cry. All I wanted was for her to feel like she had a home, and somehow convince her that I wasn't going to just toss her out after a few days.

She fought the tears and brushed them off her face. I decided to breeze on past that part of the conversation and move on to something less emotional for her.

"I have to go to work. What do you want to do while I'm

there? You can come with me. Or you're welcome to just hang around here and relax a bit," I said.

"Actually," Maya said, scooping up another bite of cheese-covered scrambled eggs, "I think I'm going to go try to find a job for myself."

"Really?" I asked.

She straightened a bit and looked at me strangely. "Well, yeah. I mean, I can't just expect to mooch off of you. If I'm going to be here for a little while, I need work. Unless you've changed your mind and don't want me staying here."

"Of course not," I said quickly. "I want you here. For as long as you want to be here. I just thought maybe you would want to take some time to relax and deal with everything before you dove right back into another job is all."

"No," she said. "I don't want to sit around because that's when I start thinking sad thoughts, and both of us know that's not something I need to be doing right now. I would rather just pick myself up, dust myself off, and try to move ahead. Getting a job will make me feel secure again."

"Well, if that's how you feel, then I'm happy to help you however I can," I said. "You said you were working at Marshall's dad's place when you were in Shelby?"

"Yeah," she said, sounding regretful. "When we got out of school, he got me a job there at the warehouse. I thought it was a fantastic idea for the two of us to be able to work together. And it was an opportunity to move up through the company. I was hoping to eventually get to design cabinets, then move on to designing furniture. Obviously, I didn't get that far."

"Well, unfortunately, you probably won't be able to find work like that around Charlotte. I can't think of any cabinet factories or warehouses around here," I said.

"I don't need to do the same thing," Maya said. "As I'm

starting over here in Charlotte, I might as well start over completely. Try something new and see where it takes me."

I gave her the rundown of the area and a few businesses she might want to try. In the back of my mind, I thought of Vince Freeman. His main job was acting CEO of Freeman Racing, but he also owned several other businesses throughout Charlotte. Restaurants, bakeries, a nightclub, and a couple of little shops made up his portfolio. He didn't have a lot to do with the day-to-day running of most of them but stayed in control and kept them profitable.

I didn't want to immediately mention him to Maya. I didn't want to build her hope up if there wasn't going to be any position available at his places. I also didn't want to take advantage of the closeness I had with the Freeman family to start promising help to other people. I would wait until she did some exploring on her own, then if she didn't have any luck, I would see what I could do.

After breakfast, I got dressed and ready for work. When I came back out to the living room, she was also dressed and was sitting in the living room putting on makeup. She looked at me out of the corner of her eye as she held up her compact and put on mascara.

"I hope you don't mind. The lighting in the bathroom wasn't very good. If I'm looking for a job, I want to make sure I don't look crazy," she said.

I laughed. "I don't mind, but we can get better lighting in the bathroom if you want. We can just change out the light bulbs. That might help." I handed her a sticky note. "There. I wrote down my work cell number and the number to the garage. Call me if you need anything at all."

"Thank you," she said. "Hopefully, I'll be okay."

"You will be, but if you need me, don't hesitate to call.

And if you really need me, you can always come by the compound."

"I wouldn't want to upset your boss," she said. "I didn't come here to cause any trouble for you."

"You wouldn't be causing any trouble," I said. "Quentin, the brother who actually owns the company, doesn't mind at all. And neither does Gus. Or Vince. Or Darren."

Maya laughed. "Is that the whole family Gus was talking about yesterday?"

"Yeah. Quentin owns the company; Vince and Darren, who you met yesterday, work there. There's one more brother, Nick, but he doesn't work for the company. He's an investor," I said.

"It's nice to see a family that close," Maya said.

"It really is," I said. "And you haven't even met Minnie, Gus's wife. Merry and Kelly, Quentin's and Darren's wives, work there, too. And Nick's best friend, Lindsey, is engaged to Vince."

"Wow," Maya said. "Way to keep everybody together."

"And the best part? They actually all do love each other. They have family dinners every week and are always doing things together," I said. "They've kind of brought me in as an honorary brother, so I get to enjoy it, too. It's a family like I've never known."

I felt a little guilty saying that, considering how much my mother had gone through to come take care of me while I was hurt. She had always been there for me, but the truth was, she was pretty much it. There was no such thing as the big extended family or the closeness I saw in the Freemans. But I was more than happy to get a chance to experience it now.

As soon as I got to the compound, Darren and Gus both

descended on me. For as much restraint as they showed the day before, both we're brimming with questions about Maya. It wasn't long before Vince came by, too, checking to see that everything was okay. I was glad they cared, and touched they wanted to make sure she was doing fine, but I tried to detour the conversation back to our bikes. We had a race to prepare for, and I wanted to be at my best.

5

MAYA

My new beginning wasn't off to the best start. I woke up that morning so optimistic and having breakfast with Greg gave me the boost I needed. He was so confident, so settled already with having me there. There wasn't a hint of hesitation or uncertainty in how he talked to me. He didn't even seem concerned about saying he wanted to add me on to the lease and have me stick around.

It was like we hadn't spent five years apart. We were picking right back where we left off like I'd seen him the week before and was just joining up with him and Charlotte. It made me feel ready to find out where life was going to take me next. He even seemed optimistic about me being able to find work fairly easily. The description of the town and the list of businesses he gave me made it seem like there were abundant opportunities just waiting for me to discover them.

I headed out in my daddy's old truck, ready to scoop up the potential and find the spot that would be best for me. It was waiting out there, and I just had to find it. Grab the bull by the horns, as my daddy would have said.

By the middle of the morning, I was wondering if I was just missing the horns. At lunchtime when I went back by the apartment to get something to eat, I was wondering why the bull was avoiding me. And by the time late afternoon had come along, I was all but sure there was no bull at all.

I had spent all day driving around Charlotte to all the places Greg mentioned, looking for open positions. When none of them panned out, I resorted to checking windows for "help wanted" signs. I found a couple, but, like Greg said, nothing even close to the warehouse.

This wasn't going to stop me, though. I hadn't worked anywhere but the warehouse for a few years, but my first job had been at a little shop in Shelby. The "help wanted" signs happened to be on two small stores, so I went in and applied at both. Best-case scenario, I would get both of them and would be able to arrange my hours so I could work both consistently and build up my savings while contributing to Greg's expenses until I was ready to head off on my own.

Worst-case scenario, I would get neither one of them, and I would be right back where I started. Considering that neither of the shop owners looked particularly impressed by me and put my application aside without even looking at it, I wasn't feeling hugely optimistic about the whole situation.

What I was feeling was despondent. I had used up every bit of optimism I had and was left feeling empty and crushed. On my way back to the apartment, I noticed a bar. An early dinner and a few drinks were well deserved after everything I had gone through.

I parked along the side of the road and went in. It was still fairly early, so there weren't many people inside. But I could smell food cooking, which meant I could grab a meal to counteract the drinks I planned on having. Rather than taking up one of the tables and emphasizing the fact that I was completely alone, I slid onto one of the barstools.

Almost as soon as I sat down, a pretty woman with her hair up in a bouncy ponytail and wide, friendly eyes came up to me. She placed a napkin in front of me.

"Can I get you something to drink?" she asked.

"Do you have any good beer on tap?"

"Sure," she said. "There's a new local craft brew I just added today."

"Sounds good," I said.

I sagged against the top of the bar as she filled a mug and put it on a napkin. She eyed me suspiciously.

"You okay?" she asked.

"It's been a long day," I said, picking up the beer and taking a sip.

"You hungry?"

I nodded. "Something smells good."

"Do you have anything particular you're in the mood for?" she asked.

I shook my head and took another sip of the delicious craft brew. "No. Just hungry."

A faint smile curved her lips. It was one of those compassionate expressions, an empathetic look from a woman who could probably recognize my downtrodden expression.

"Let me grab you something. I'll be right back," she said.

She left me alone sitting at the bar, and I looked around, taking it all in. This was the kind of place I could see people in the neighborhood wanting to relax and enjoy themselves. It had a good feeling about it. I looked over to the side and something caught my eye. A picture propped next to the cash register looked familiar. I sat up a bit so I could get a better look at it, and the bartender caught me.

She gave me a strange look as she set the plate down at my stool.

"I'm sorry," I said, sitting back down. "That picture just looked familiar."

She glanced back at it, then at me. "You know those guys?"

"I just met Darren yesterday," I said. "But Greg has been my best friend since I was a kid. I don't know the other guys."

"Seriously? Greg is your best friend?" she asked.

"Yeah. Right up until he left Shelby. I'm actually here staying with him for a bit."

She grinned widely and stepped back to the picture. She pointed at one of the guys I didn't recognize. "This is Quentin. He's the one who owns the company. This one is Nick—he's *my* best friend. And this is Vince. My fiancé."

Realization settled in. "Oh. You're Lindsey. Greg told me about you." I laughed. "I can't believe I managed to come in here on my own. I had no idea you work here."

"Greg didn't send you in?"

I popped one of the perfectly fried French fries into my mouth and shook my head. "No. He doesn't even know I'm here. He's been at work all day."

Lindsey laughed and nodded. "Yep. That sounds like all the boys. Greg might not have been born a Freeman, but he fits right in with them. I think that's why the only man I could realistically see myself having a future with was a Freeman. I was already so used to them through Nick, I just slid right into the lifestyle."

I nodded. "I can understand that."

She was wiping down the counter but kept glancing

over at me. I kept eating until she stepped back closer and refilled my beer.

"So, what brings you to Charlotte? Just coming to hang out with Greg?" she asked.

There was a hint in her voice that suggested she had never heard about me and was wondering how I managed to resurface. It didn't really bother me. He'd left Shelby for a reason, and I could understand him wanting to leave everything about it behind, too.

"Actually, I'm staying for a while. I just went through a pretty nasty breakup."

"I feel you on that," she said sympathetically. "Were you two together for a long time?"

"Marshall and I were together for three years," I told her. "We weren't engaged or anything. We had just moved in together. Apparently, that pushed him right over the edge. I wouldn't know, considering he didn't give me any explanation at all, but one day he just came home and told me it was over, and I needed to leave. I then promptly found out I no longer had a job at the warehouse his father owns that I've been working at for three years." I realized what I had just done and let out a sigh. "I'm sorry. You don't need me babbling to you."

"I don't mind," she said. "You sound like you could use somebody to talk to." She leaned a little closer. "It's part of being a bartender. Besides, Greg is a friend of mine, which means you are, too. Feel free to vent however much you want."

I took her at her word and poured out everything to her. I told her about my relationship with Marshall and how suddenly it ended. Then I told her about losing my job and not feeling like I had anywhere to go, so I ended up here with Greg.

"I'm pretty lucky to have had him to come to," I said. "Honestly, I don't know what I would have done if I didn't."

"He's a really good guy," Lindsey said.

"Yes, he is," I said, finishing my second beer. Lindsey took the mug and filled it up again. "Which makes me feel even worse."

"What do you mean?" Lindsey asked.

"I went out today to find a job so I could earn my keep. I didn't want to just show up at his place and expect him to support me while I figured out what I was supposed to do next. But I haven't been able to find anything. I filled out two applications, but I'm not exactly running out for work clothes, if you know what I mean," I said.

"How do you feel about kitchens?" Lindsey asked.

I gave her a strange look. "Just in general? Or a particular kind of kitchen?"

"Like the one here at the bar," she said. "How would you feel about working here?"

"Seriously?"

"Yeah."

"Is the owner looking for somebody?" I asked.

"Well, let me ask just to make sure," Lindsey said. She turned slightly to the side and cocked her hip. "Are you looking for somebody to work in the kitchen?" She turned the other direction and talked to the other hip. "Yeah, I think that it would be really good to have some extra help." She turned back the other way. "Great. I'll let her know."

"You own the bar?" I asked, feeling stupid.

"Yeah," she said with a grin. "This is my place. I inherited it from my father. So I can tell you with pretty good authority there's a position open."

"Please don't take my getting through three beers

during my conversation with you as an indication of my character," I said.

Lindsey laughed. "I won't. Like I said, it's just a job in the kitchen. I'm going to be really honest with you. It's low pay and crappy hours to start, but if you show results and trust, and you fit in well around here, you can move up easily. Especially considering we're starting to think about expanding a bit. The restaurant side of the place is getting more popular, and I'm thinking about adding on."

"That sounds amazing," I said. Then I thought about it. "Wait. Do you have cherry pie on your menu?"

Lindsey narrowed her eyes at me slightly. "No."

I let out a sigh and smiled. "Good. Then I can definitely help. And I promise I won't let you down."

6

GREG

I hadn't heard from Maya all day, and it was starting to worry me. I figured she would keep me updated throughout the day while she looked for a job. When we'd talked about it over breakfast, she seemed optimistic about finding work and settling in. She didn't want to just coast, even though I would have been fine with it if she did want to take some time to decompress.

I wouldn't have blamed her if she didn't want to jump right back into the normal grind of life. After the shock and disappointment of what she went through, it would make sense for her to be angry. A lot of people would want some time to just clear their heads and try to figure out what life was going to be like moving forward.

After three years with Marshall, Maya needed to figure out who she was on her own. There was a big difference between being twenty years old, still in college, and just working out the details of life, and three years later. Not that those three years had aged her beyond recognition, but people did a lot of learning and changing during those years.

I was perfectly willing to be there for her. When I said she could come stay with me and I'd get her added to the lease, it was because I wanted to help her. She needed somebody now more than ever. Even though we'd spent five years apart, I still considered her extremely special. Those few years didn't change everything we'd gone through together, and I wasn't going to leave her dangling when she needed me the most.

Maya seemed ready to jump right into her next chapter, or at the very least ready to forget about the last one by distracting herself. I figured she would let me know how she was doing throughout the day, or at least tell me where she was applying for jobs. By the end of the day, I hadn't even gotten so much as a text from her.

Maybe she had changed her mind, and after I left for work, she decided to just relax for the day. It wasn't uncommon for me to hang out at the compound for a few hours after the official workday was over, but that day I started getting ready to leave as early as possible. I wanted to get back to the apartment and make sure Maya was alright.

I parked in front of the building with a nervous feeling in my stomach. She was a mess when she'd first showed up at the compound but seemed oddly put together that morning. Maybe a bit too put together. I worried I'd walk into the apartment and find her having suddenly come to the realization of what was happening in her life and falling apart.

I would do anything I could to help her and make her feel better, but I didn't know if I was totally prepared to see her like that. Maya and I had helped each other through a lot when we were younger, but a life-changing breakup wasn't one of those things. I prepared myself with as many of the comforting statements and platitudes as I possibly could, then headed inside.

"Hey," Maya said when I got inside. "You're home earlier than I thought you'd be. How was your day at work?"

She didn't just sound okay. She sounded downright perky. I didn't know if that was a good thing, or if I should be more worried about her. I walked into the living room where she was reclined on the couch with a beer in her hand. The rest of a six-pack sat on the coffee table in front of her next to a restaurant to-go bag.

"It was pretty good," I said. "Just kind of same old same old."

She laughed. "Somehow, I can't imagine working on a motorcycle racing complex could ever be just same old same old. But I guess anything can become routine if you do it enough. Come on, sit down. I was just getting ready to watch a movie."

She didn't look sad or like she had disconnected with reality, so I plopped down beside her and reached for one of the beers. I grabbed the bottle opener and popped the cap on the bottle before tossing both back to the table. Maya waited while I took a deep swig, then picked up the white paper bag.

"What's that?" I asked.

"I brought you dinner," she said. "I had the same thing. It was really good."

I looked at the bag and noticed it was from Lindsey's bar. "You ended up at Lindsey's?" I asked. "Did you get to meet her?"

"I did," she said. "She's really nice. I didn't even realize who she was when I went into the bar. I wasn't exactly having the best day, and I went in there to grab a drink. Then I got a job."

She slipped that into the conversation so seamlessly I nearly dropped the burger I had unwrapped from its white waxed paper. Finishing the bite, I wiped my lips and stared at her. My eyebrows pulled together as I tried to figure out if she was being serious or if there was some sort of joke I'd missed along the line.

"I think I missed a step," I said.

Maya laughed. "That's how I felt, too. The whole day was kind of a bust. I went to all the places you told me to look, but nobody was hiring. Apparently, there was some sort of employment boom around Charlotte. None of the business owners needed more staff. Either that, or they took one look at me, saw me as an outsider, and decided they weren't going to give me a job."

I laughed and shook my head, taking another bite of the burger. It was delicious, but that was no surprise. Lindsey was known for making the best burgers in town. She even had a special one she'd created in honor of Nick Freeman, her best friend.

"I don't think that was the case," I said. "Something like that might have happened in Shelby, but Charlotte isn't that kind of small town. So, you didn't find anywhere that was hiring? How did you get a job?"

"Well, I found two little stores that were hiring. I figured I had some experience with work like that. Remember that gift shop I worked at in high school?" she asked.

"Yeah," I said. "It was the only place that would hire you when you were fourteen. Of course, that was probably because they never got any customers, so you didn't really have to do anything."

"They got some customers," Maya argued.

"Maybe a few, but if those stores need you to actually be

able to interact with people or run a cash register, you might not be the best choice," I said.

Maya gave me an aggravated look and shook her head. "Well, that doesn't really matter. I filled out applications for both of those, but they didn't seem very motivated to hire me. That's actually how I ended up in the bar. I was feeling kind of bummed and figured I deserved a drink and maybe an early dinner. You had mentioned you sometimes stay at the compound late, so I didn't know when you were going to be back."

"I guess that's as good an excuse as any," I said. "But how did you know it was Lindsey's place? I don't even think I mentioned to you that she owns a bar."

"You didn't," Maya said. "I was sitting there at the bar feeling sorry for myself, and she came up to talk to me. She brought me a beer and some food, and I noticed a picture next to the cash register."

"The one up on the mirror?" I asked.

"Yeah, that one. I pointed it out, and she told me who she was. So, I told her how I ended up in Charlotte, and the whole messy story just kind of came out."

I nodded. "Lindsey's a really good listener. She can get anybody to open up about anything. And the best part about it is that she usually has a way to make people feel better."

"Well, she definitely did this time. She asked me if I would be okay working in a kitchen, which would be the point in the conversation when I humiliated myself by asking her if the owner of the bar was actually looking for help," Maya said.

I laughed. "That's okay. She's used to it. A lot of people around here still think of it as her father's bar."

"She was understanding about it. Then she offered me a

job. It's nothing glamorous or anything. It's low pay and crappy hours. Her words, not mine. But she mentioned I would have room for moving up if I did well. So, that's what my day was. I got a job and a really good burger," Maya said. "Oh, and got a ride home from my new boss because I had three beers before she offered me the job. So, memorable first impression achieved."

"I would say that's a pretty successful first day in Charlotte," I said.

She smiled at me. "I would, too. Thank you for encouraging me."

I put my burger down on the coffee table and pulled Maya in for a tight hug. I was so happy for her. I came home worried I would find her an absolute wreck and not know how to help her through it. Now she seemed ready for what was ahead. Or, at least, ready to give it a try.

"Good things will happen here, I promise," I said. "It's such a great town."

"It has to be," she said. "You chose it, and you stayed here for this long. It has to have something to offer."

"It does. You'll see. and I'm excited to show it all to you," I said.

"Well, I feel like maybe I've had enough new and exciting things for the day. I was thinking we could go back in time a bit this evening," she said.

She reached for the remote and hit the Play button. One of our favorite movies from when we were teenagers came on the screen, and I laughed.

"That's a throwback," I said. "How many times did we watch this thing?"

"About a thousand," she said. "All that old furniture down in the basement was the one good thing about having to stay with my aunt and uncle all the time."

That brought back a lot of memories, but not all of them were ones we wanted to dwell on. Both of us had ghosts in our past. They were what brought us together, but I was more than happy to just keep them behind me.

We settled in for the movie. When I was done with my burger, I went to the kitchen and made popcorn. We followed up the first movie with another, and by the time it was over, I was getting tired.

"I'm going to take a shower," I told her. "I need to get some sleep."

I got up and mussed her hair, smiling to myself as I walked away. Having my best friend in town was going to be great. If only I could convince myself I'd let her go when she was ready.

7

MAYA

I woke up early the next morning and lay there on the couch, staring up at the ceiling. I really didn't have any reason to be up that early. I wasn't starting my new job at Lindsey's bar until the next Monday, but even when I did, my hours wouldn't start until the late afternoon.

I couldn't go back to sleep. I wasn't anxious or particularly unhappy. This wasn't the kind of being awake that usually left me tossing and turning trying to go back to sleep. I didn't feel any sort of lingering negativity from a nightmare I might have woken up from and forgotten. Instead, it just felt like my mind was ready to start my day. I got up and walked quietly into the bathroom to take a shower.

Greg didn't have much longer to sleep, and I didn't want to disturb him. From what I'd watched during the day I'd spent at the compound with him, he worked hard. He needed good, solid sleep to be in top shape. And knowing Greg, he didn't get that sleep as often as he really needed it.

From the time we were kids, if he got his mind on something, he didn't let go. He would push and push until he ground himself into exhaustion to make sure he achieved what was in front of him. He had told me all about the horrific accident he'd had and how it took him out of racing for an entire season.

It was enough to motivate him to push as hard as he possibly could to get back into his best form. Greg wouldn't just settle for recovering. He wanted to be better than he ever was. He wanted to prove to everybody that the crash hadn't ruined him and that he would go on to achieve everything he would have if he had never had that accident.

After my shower, I got dressed and twisted my wet hair up on the back of my head to secure with a clip.

Once I was dressed and ready for the day, I went into the kitchen and started searching through all of Greg's cabinets and his refrigerator and freezer. It was surprisingly well-stocked for a bachelor who lived alone. Being around all those domesticated Freemans all the time must have been a good influence on him.

Suddenly inspired, I pulled out a few armfuls of ingredients and spread them across the wide counter along the far wall. Finding the right pots and pans wasn't the quietest of endeavors, and I was sure I had woken Greg up.

Sure enough, a couple of minutes later, I heard the shower running in the bathroom. Greg came into the kitchen a while later, rubbing sleep out of his eyes and yawning wide.

"Did I wake you?" I asked. "I'm sorry."

"It's okay," he said. "I needed to get up, anyway. Last night was just a late night. What are you doing in here?"

He was looking at everything I was working on suspiciously.

"I'm making breakfast," I told him.

"For how many people?" he asked.

I laughed. "Well, I'm making breakfast and a couple of other things, too. I found a bunch of really great things in your kitchen and got inspired. I have breakfast burritos with sausage, eggs, cheese, peppers, and onions cooking for you it to bring to work for everybody."

I walked over to the counter and swiped my finger across the screen of my phone where I had it propped up. Checking the recipe that showed up, I measured out a few more ingredients and added them to the mixing bowl in front of me.

"What are you working on there?" he asked. "That looks suspiciously like baking."

I laughed.

"It is, actually."

"Should I brace myself for disaster?" he asked.

"Maybe," I said. "But I'm feeling pretty optimistic about this one. I found a good recipe for banana walnut muffins, and they just sounded delicious. You had a few really ripe bananas in your fruit bowl, so it seemed like the perfect opportunity."

"I'm sorry," Greg said. "I came in here looking for my best friend. Maybe you know her. Maya Klein? Cute little thing, big eyes, dark hair, tragedy in all things baking?"

I made a mock gasp, but then nodded. "Yep, that's me."

"Then what's going on? What's prompted this cooking frenzy?"

I shrugged. "I don't know. It's weird. I just woke up this morning feeling like I had another chance. Does that make sense? Like moving here wasn't just about getting away from Shelby or Marshall. It's about having a whole new experience with life. And maybe I shouldn't just keep going with the way I have always thought of myself. Like I get to be whoever I want to be now."

"And who you want to be is someone who makes breakfast burritos by the dozen?" Greg asked, pouring himself coffee and looking at me like he wasn't following me completely.

"I don't know. Maybe. But the point is, I can try. I can do all these things I've avoided, or I've thought of myself as being bad at, and see if maybe something can change."

"I can respect that," Greg said. "That was pretty much what I did when I came to Charlotte. I put as much of my past behind me as I could, and I started a new life. So, other than making the biggest breakfast known to man, what are you doing today?"

"Nothing that I had plans for," I said. "I don't start working until Monday, so the next few days are pretty much open."

"Great. Come back to the compound with me. I want to introduce you around to the people you didn't get to meet," he said.

"Sure," I said. "I'll bring the burritos and muffins."

I had always found that sharing food was the fastest way to make new friends, and that's exactly what I wanted to do. I trusted Greg and his evaluation of people. If this circle were his friends, then that's where I wanted to be.

When we first got to the complex, I saw Darren and Gus again. A woman was there with Darren, and Greg introduced me to Kelly, Darren's wife. She was a mechanic there, working on the race bikes and also building custom ones for customers. She was friendly and seemed sweet and down-to-earth. We talked throughout the day, and I found myself really liking her.

I was having such a good time watching Greg work and getting to know everybody around the garage that I was surprised when it was already time for lunch. We walked up to a large, sprawling field in the middle of the compound. Several other people were arriving from other angles as we walked up. An elegant-looking woman in a long sundress walked over to a long picnic table and added several containers of food to the ones already sitting there.

"Do you guys eat lunch together every day?" I asked Greg.

"Pretty much," he said. "It started with them just ordering a time or two a week, but then we enjoyed eating together so much that it just became something Minnie and Gus do for us."

"Hey, Greg," a woman cradling a baby said as she came from the direction of the main complex buildings. "How are you doing?"

"Hey, Merry. Doing well. Really excited about the race tomorrow. Meet Maya," Greg said.

The woman's eyes lit up, and she extended a hand to me. "Maya. I've heard about you. You and Greg you are old friends, yes?"

It made me feel good that he had at least talked about me to somebody in Charlotte. I nodded.

"Yeah," I said. "We are."

Greg smiled. "Maya has always been my best friend." Our eyes met for a brief second before he turned his attention back to the woman and gestured toward her. "Merry is Quentin's wife. This is their little girl, Ruby."

"It's nice to meet you," I said.

"You too. Are you hungry? This looks amazing. Let's grab something to eat."

Greg gave an encouraging nod, and I followed Merry to the table with the food. That started an hour and a half of meeting people and finding out about the life Greg had been living in the five years since we'd last seen each other. It was strange in a way.

Part of me immediately felt jealous. He was *my* Greg, after all. We had known each other our whole lives. We'd been inseparable when we got a little older. Hearing them talk about him and their memories with him when I wasn't around felt like an intrusion.

At the same time, they were all so nice and inclusive it was hard not to like them. And Greg was happy around them. I loved that they had welcomed him, that he felt comfortable and accepted by them, and they were doing everything they could to make me feel the same way. Minnie, the matriarch of the Freeman family, swept me up in a hug as soon as she met me. All the brothers took a few moments to ask after me, and the women offered me their babies to hold while we talked.

As someone who grew up in the circumstances I had, I was overwhelmed, but in the best way. It was that kind of overwhelmed when you get too many birthday presents or see Santa Claus for the first time. It was too much, but I didn't want less. I could definitely see why Greg said they were such a great family to work for.

When we left that night, it was with hugs from everybody I'd met. They gushed about the food I brought and asked me to bring more. That made me smile, and I couldn't wipe the grin off my face even ten minutes later when we were driving down the road. Greg looked over at me and mirrored the smile.

"You look happy," he said.

"I just can't believe they liked the food I made," I said. "Sounds silly, but that really means a lot to me."

"It should," Greg said. "Especially coming from them. Minnie cooks all the time. And I mean all the time. That place is constantly full of baked goods she makes. They are pretty particular, and they wouldn't lie about liking something."

"Do you think we could stop by the grocery store?" I asked.

"Sure, do you need something?"

"I want to stock up on ingredients. I have a whole list of recipes I want to try. And I have the time to do it, so why not?" I asked.

He grinned a little wider. "Why not?"

8

GREG

I could definitely get used to waking up in the morning to the smells of Maya making breakfast. Even if those smells were often accompanied by loud music playing and creative streams of profanity when she knocked over pots and pans or burned something. Her new life quest might be to conquer baking, but like most life quests, it wasn't going to be instantly successful.

Even with the missteps, I was impressed by her dedication. It might seem like a small thing to a lot of people, but her sudden devotion to baking was a big step. It carried a lot more meaning to me than her just wanting to be able to whip up a nice basket of muffins when she was planning on visiting.

This was about her overcoming perceptions of herself and challenges she faced when we were young. This was one of the things about her I knew most people she encountered never knew. She was sweet and fun and beautiful, and people often thought of her as being carefree.

I knew that wasn't really the case. Not that she was fake in any way. Just that she chose what she was willing to show to other people. And that very rarely included the darkness that still hung over her from her past.

The deaths of her parents and everything she went through after were extremely hard on her. Instead of letting herself struggle with those issues directly, she instead developed different ways of channeling the pain. Unfortunately, that came in the form of her limiting herself.

She pushed back against commitment and closeness to people with a vengeance. She often teased herself for not living up to ideals, or her being bad at very specific things. Sometimes she was right, but other times, I felt like she was depending on those limitations to be her scapegoat.

If she said she didn't want a commitment or didn't want to be a wife and mother, she didn't have to risk opening her heart to someone who would hurt her. She didn't have to face the fear that she might end up not being a good mother or leaving her child too soon.

If she could say she was really bad at baking, then she didn't have to face it and possibly get a recipe wrong or make something people didn't like. Baking meant more to her than just cooking. She was willing to cook because it came naturally to her, but baking felt more significant. She always said people put so much emphasis on baked goods. Birthday and wedding cakes. Special treats on holidays.

Baking felt more like handing her heart over to somebody. Her mother baked when she was young. She never believed she could live up to that.

Seeing her suddenly motivated to try these new things and face the discomfort and fear she always felt made me hopeful. It was like she really was willing to start this new life. She was going to put Marshall and all that nonsense behind her and discover who she could really be.

That Thursday morning, I woke up to a towering stack

of blueberry pancakes and another studded with chocolate chips. Bacon made a mountain on another, and she was staring down into a pot of what I could only imagine would eventually be hard-boiled eggs.

"Smells good," I said when I walked into the kitchen and headed for the coffee maker.

"Thanks," she said. "I'm making you a couple of snacks to bring to work with you. All that junk food you have stuffed in your locker isn't good for you."

I laughed. "See? This is what I get for having a woman in my house. All of a sudden I can't eat cheese doodles anymore."

She shook her head and waved a spoon at me. "Nope. No cheese doodles for you."

"So, should I go ahead and throw away the bag you have hidden in the cabinet under the TV?" I asked.

"Also, nope," she said. "Those don't count. Movie food."

I nodded, accepting her logic. "So, tonight is the race. I'm not going to the compound; I'm meeting up with the team and heading right for the track. You should come. It's a lot of fun."

It was true. The races were a blast, but I also just didn't want to leave her alone in her first week in Charlotte. I didn't want her to feel abandoned or like she wasn't a part of everything. Somehow, she didn't seem bothered. Instead, she shook her head.

"No that's ok, I'm going to just hang around here. I only have a few more days until I have to start work, so I plan on spoiling myself with a bubble bath, hours of cooking shows, and baking. I was thinking about cooking up some freezer meals, so you'll be all stocked up for weeknight dinners."

"That sounds good. But you know I have to put in a request," I said.

She looked over her shoulder at me. "Your favorite? Black forest cake?"

"Absolutely," I said. "You need to get that one down pat. I'll be requiring them on at least a monthly basis."

Maya laughed and wrapped her arms around me in a tight hug. "Have a good race. But be careful. I don't want to get a call from anybody that you're smeared across the track. I just don't have time for all that."

I grinned and gave her a squeeze. "I promise. And I'll give you a call when I'm done and headed back to the apartment. It might be kind of late."

"That's fine. I'll be around. Good luck and be safe," she said.

When I got to the racetrack, the first thing the team did was help set up the tailgate party. This was one of Merry's brilliant ideas. Along with being Quentin's wife, she was also the Freeman Racing's social media manager and PR consultant.

What started as her just revamping the team's social media presence and working to build more of an online presence turned into full-blown marketing. She was brimming with ideas for how to build the team's fanbase even more and attract the attention of bigger and more impressive sponsors. And this was particularly important for me. I didn't have the Freeman name to fall back on. If I wanted to be anything more than just the second rider on their team, I had to build a reputation for myself.

The tailgate parties before the races were working well to get me there. The parties drew crowds of fans to eat from local food trucks, listen to music, and buy special race-specific merchandise. There was also an exhibit demonstrating the custom-bike service offered as a side business to the main racing company.

During my time away because of my injuries, the parties were focused on Darren. However as soon as I was able to get back out on the track, they introduced me back into them. Now both of us had fans who came to buy T-shirts and get autographs. We took pictures and chatted for a few minutes before it was time to head down to the track.

It was always a boost to have that bit of time with our fans. It reminded us even more why we loved our careers so much.

As much as we enjoyed the parties, we never let ourselves stay too long. The most important part of getting to the racetrack early was it allowed Darren and me to walk down to the track itself. This was a ritual he and I had done from the very beginning. The day of my first race, he walked with me down to the track, and we stepped out onto it.

Rather than just looking at it, we walked around the entire thing. Taking a lap around the oval before getting on our bikes was a way to get the feel of it, to get used to it and see it from a different perspective. It helped us later when we were zipping around at a hundred miles an hour. We weren't in a rush when we walked around, but taking that time pumped us up and made us feel more prepared.

It was also a chance to just talk. There wasn't any one specific topic we talked about, and though it might have seemed counterintuitive, we always avoided talking about the race. It was almost like we wanted that lap around the track to feel normal, to integrate it into our regular thoughts so it felt more familiar to us later.

We had already raced on this particular track many times, but I still enjoyed the chance to walk around it. That day, our conversation went right to Maya.

"How do you think she's settling in?" Darren asked.

"Well, it's only been a couple of days, but she seems to be doing all right. Of course, the whole thing was a major shock to her at first, but I feel like her coming here was the best thing possible for her. She can get away from all the mess in Shelby and really start over."

"Like you did?" Darren asked.

"Exactly," I said. "You know, we haven't seen each other since I left. I'm really glad that didn't stop her from coming to me when she needed help. It doesn't matter to me how long we're apart. I would do anything for Maya."

"Sounds like it," Darren said. "The two of you are really close, aren't you?"

"Closer than any other person in my life," I said. "I can't really explain it. But we kind of buffer each other from the world. No matter what we were going through, we were always able to fall back on each other. We were safe when we were together. What was funny about it was we didn't have the same group of friends, or the same interests. Other than things like watching the same movies."

"Then how did you end up such good friends?" Darren asked.

"Honestly, I don't really know. We've known each other pretty much our entire lives. Shelby isn't a big place, so you're bound to interact with most people who live there. But we didn't really become close until the end of middle school. We just kind of started spending time together. Then we spent more time together. Then that was it," I said. "We had our own little bubble away from everything and everyone else."

"So, how well do you really know her?" Darren asked, the question heavy with a second meaning.

I threw a glare at him. "Not like that. I don't know her that way at all."

"Seriously?" Darren asked. "You two are that close, you talk about her like you would lay down your life for her, but you've never, you know, *been* with her?"

"Never," I said.

"Seriously? Never?" he asked.

"Not at all," I said. "It wasn't like that with Maya and me. And I didn't bring her to live with me because of that." Though if I were honest with myself, I wouldn't be upset if it happened.

"I know that," Darren said. "You just want what's best for her. I think it's amazing that she got a job at Lindsey's place. We all really like her, Greg. We want to take care of her just like we do you."

The conversation I had with Darren made me feel good, and I carried that feeling with me into the race that night. I came in second to Darren. Even though I didn't win, I couldn't be disappointed in placing second in my first race back after my injury."

Coming in second still gave me a solid payday on top of the bonuses the sponsors gave me. It would pad my bank account even more and let me help Maya get what she needed to settle into her new life. Starting with buying her an actual bed.

As I stood there getting my prize and posing for pictures, all I could think about was calling her and telling her about my win. I couldn't help, but wish she were there.

9

MAYA

Having the apartment to myself while Greg was out at the race felt luxurious. His place was much nicer than the one I'd been living in before moving in with Marshall.

One of the things about Marshall that had impressed me and made me feel like I could have a relationship with him was that he seemed so much more humble than the rest of his family. I knew when we were in high school, he had the reputation of being like the other Brinkleys, which meant he was known for being arrogant and elitist. I didn't see that in him. He was kind and generous when we started dating, and he went to great lengths not to be associated with his father when working at the factory.

And it kept him from living in as much luxury as he had the option to. Even still, his apartment was beautiful, and when I got to move into it, I felt like I was on top of the world. I had really arrived. Or at least I was definitely on my way.

Yet I never fully settled in there. I was comfortable in

that apartment. We had spent a lot of time together there when we were dating, and I was familiar with it. When I moved in, I put a lot of effort into making it as much my own as I could. But by the time I left, it still didn't feel like home. I had tried to tell myself it was because it had only been a few weeks. I knew now that I'd been wrong.

Being here with Greg was different. I had only been living in his apartment for a few days and was still sleeping on a couch in a spare room. Yet, I felt more comfortable and at ease in that space than I ever had in Marshall's apartment.

Despite feeling so comfortable and looking forward to the chance to cook and relax, I felt a little bit guilty for not going to the race. For everything Greg was doing for me, the least I could do in return was be there to support him while he raced. But the thought terrified me.

I had watched racing in my life. I'd even gone to a few car races and found myself having fun, all swept up in the excitement and enthusiasm at the events. Still it was such an abstract idea to me. It was just nameless, faceless people driving around. I wasn't really there for the mindless circling of the track.

I was there for the music, the beer, and the dancing. The races were fun, but when I thought about Greg being one of the people out there on the track, not even in a car, but on the back of a motorcycle, it made my heart tighten in my stomach flip. I was terrified something was going to happen to him.

The story of his crash was horrifying. When he first told me about it, I tried to laugh my way through it. I tried to make it seem like it wasn't a big deal. If I shrugged it off and didn't let myself really think about it, then I didn't have to be so afraid. I didn't have to have the terror and sadness thinking about him going through that much danger and pain.

There was no way I would be able to stand there and watch him race. Not right now, at least. My emotions were still worn thin, and I doubted I would be able to cope with the stress and worry of watching him be right on the brink of disaster again.

This didn't mean I didn't miss him. He had only been gone for a short while when I realized I wished he was still there. It was so nice having him around. I had already gotten used to the feeling of him being in my life again.

Fortunately, I could comfort myself by diving into the bags of groceries I'd picked up at the store on the way back from the compound the day before. I might have gone a little bit overboard, but every time I turned down an aisle, I saw more ingredients that reminded me of recipes I'd found or inspired me to try something new.

Now that I'd gotten the baking bug, I couldn't stop thinking about everything I wanted to do. The conversation I'd had with Greg stuck with me. He was so surprised by how excited I was to start baking, and maybe I should have been, too. It was never my strength, but it was always something my mother did. I compared myself to her and felt like I would never be able to live up to her memory.

And now I felt like I could do it. Suddenly, it was like parts of me that had been hiding were freed and I could try to find myself again. Or maybe really be myself for the first time.

That day, I started with a few basics as a warm-up. Muffins and biscuits filled baskets on the counter, and a batch of cupcakes were already in the oven. I went over the recipe of for Greg's black forest cake and gathered up all the ingredients. With my new favorite baking show playing in the background, I mixed up the batter for the cake and poured it into the baking pans so they would be ready as soon as I took the cupcakes out of the oven.

When that was finished, it was time to face the foe that had been intimidating me for years. I was going to bake bread.

Several minutes of careful measuring, re-measuring, and measuring for a third time later, I mixed the flour, yeast, salt, sugar, and water together into what looked like the perfect dough. I dropped it down into a mixing bowl coated with oil and draped a kitchen towel over it. I had even stolen the trick of one of the TV chefs and warmed the towel in the microwave before I put it over the bowl.

Now all I had to do was wait. The bread had to rise for an hour before I could punch and knead it. I looked down at myself and realized I was completely covered with all manners of kitchen residue. Flour, chocolate, sugar, oil, and eggs coated my apron and stuck to my skin. I needed a shower.

An idea occurred to me, and I smiled. What I really needed was a bath.

There was a small bathroom off my bedroom, but it only had a walk-in shower. A quick peek into Greg's bathroom confirmed he had a nice bathtub. He wouldn't mind if I borrowed it for just a little bit while he was gone.

I sank into steaming hot water and a thick layer of bubbles. I slid down against the back wall of the tub until the bubbles covered me up to my chin. They smelled like the sweet vanilla honey body wash I'd bought at the store along with my groceries. Greg teased me when I picked it up, pointing out I was even choosing food-themed soap now.

The truth was, it used to be my favorite body wash before I started dating Marshall. Then he told me he didn't like how sweet it smelled. That it reminded him of a bakery. Somehow that was a bad thing coming from him, and I agreed to stop using it. As soon as I saw it in the store with Greg, I had to buy it. Using it again made me feel like me.

I had a timer set on my phone to stop me from just staying in the tub for the rest of the day. It allowed me a long, luxurious soak. And when I got out, I felt relaxed and calm. So relaxed and calm, in fact, I decided I was emotionally prepared to do something I had been adamantly avoiding since driving away from Shelby.

After getting dressed in a pair of leggings and a light-weight long-sleeve T-shirt, I grabbed my phone and curled up on one of the overstuffed chairs in the living room to scroll through social media. I only had a few minutes left before it was time to tend to the bread. Just that short, little bit of time couldn't hurt.

Boy, was I wrong. I had been totally boycotting all forms of social media since the breakup with Marshall, so I hadn't had a chance to erase him from my platforms.

The effort of algorithms still brought him up first as soon as I signed on. I had tried to prepare myself for that. I told myself he was probably out living it up now that I was gone. I just hadn't realized he would be living it up in quite that way.

Of course, I knew he had started dating somebody new. The migration of his clothes from the apartment in the days before he kicked me out told me as much. I hadn't noticed it, but as soon as I did, everything clicked into place. He had been working late hours and then going over to his parents' house. A couple of times, he had gone out with the guys, then told me that one person or another had a birthday or was going through something hard and needed a friendly ear.

Whatever the excuse, he figured out a way to stay away from the apartment several times in the weeks before I left. I knew that had to mean he hadn't waited to start up with somebody else.

But actually seeing it made my blood boil. What bothered me wasn't looking at a picture of him with another woman. I mean looking at a picture of him kissing another woman wouldn't be the worst either. It wasn't exactly the most comfortable thing I had ever seen in my life, but I had a feeling I would have been able to handle it far better if it hadn't been *her*.

But there she was. Ashley Pride, a woman I once considered a friend. One of the only friends I had, in fact. I thought we were fairly close, and now I was staring at a picture of her wrapped around my ex-boyfriend in shorts so short they could have been a bikini bottom and her mouth open so far it was difficult to tell whether she was kissing him or trying to consume him whole.

I also couldn't help but notice the set of keys dangling conspicuously in her hand. The caption of the picture spoke volumes.

"Moving Day!"

I didn't know how to react. I didn't know if I should cry or throw up. Or maybe throw up and cry. Or throw things, then cry, then throw up. I ended up taking it all out on the bread. Dumping the dough out onto the flour-dusted counter, I pounded and kneaded it into oblivion. Then I started up another batch. I would have to wait for it to rise, but I had a feeling the anger wasn't going to go away within the next hour.

By the time I went to bed around two in the morning, I had a lot of bread, but only a little less anger.

10

GREG

After the race on Thursday, we all went out like we usually did. When we were close to home, we went to Lindsey's bar. This time we were just far enough out that by the time we were all packed up and would have gotten back to the bar, it would have been way too late. Instead, we found a little local bar and went there for a couple of rounds of celebratory drinks. I called Maya, but she didn't answer. It was pretty late, so I figured she had already gone to bed.

The celebration ended up going well into the night, and one-too-many celebratory rounds meant no one wanted me driving home by myself. Instead, Vince, the ever-responsible Freeman, took over driving the truck and brought me to his house for the night. I texted Maya to let her know I wouldn't be home, and she sent back a simple "okay."

I felt guilty for ditching her, but at the same time, she was settling in well, and it was probably good for her to have a chance to just enjoy some time to herself. By the next morning, I still hadn't heard from her, so I figured she was coping just fine on her own. Usually the compound was closed the day after a race, but we hadn't gotten around to unloading all of the equipment the night before.

Vince and I headed over to the garage to get unpacked, and I sent Maya a couple of text messages just keeping her updated on what was going on. She seemed perfectly fine when she messaged me back, telling me I didn't need to rush home.

We had gotten a late start to the day, and it took several hours to get everything unloaded and back in place at the compound. From there, I got wrapped up in checking over my bike and seeing how it had fared during the race. I went to work cleaning and touching it up. That led me to noticing a few things that needed adjustments, and soon I had the entire thing dismantled and spread out in the garage.

The guys insisted we break for the day when it was too dark to see clearly. They suggested we go for dinner, and I texted Maya to see if she wanted to join us. She didn't respond, so I let her know I'd be back later and headed to Lindsey's. While I was there, I made it a point to take her aside privately and thank her for giving Maya the opportunity.

"It's not much," Lindsey said. "I wish I could do more, but I'm fully staffed right now. I've been looking for somebody to help out in the kitchen, so it's a good fit. I just feel bad it's nothing more substantial for her."

"You don't need to apologize at all," I told her. "If it wasn't for you, she wouldn't have a job. She's a hard worker, and she's not the type to see anything as being beneath her. She'll do well for you."

"I look forward to working with her," Lindsey said.

By the time I got home, the apartment was quiet, and I realized Maya must have fallen asleep. I was still tired, so I took a quick shower and dropped into bed. That didn't last for long. I was blasted out of sleep just a few minutes later by the sound of Queen blaring from the kitchen.

I stumbled out of the bedroom and to the kitchen where I found Maya dancing around with a bowl under her arm. She stirred to the rhythm and wiggled her hips around, occasionally flipping her hair and singing out a jumbled line or two.

I stood there and watched her for a few seconds, and it hit me just how gorgeous she was. It wasn't a new thought either. In fact, it was one I had harbored for a long time. I just never let myself have it for long, and I definitely never said it out loud. I'd never wanted to jeopardize our friendship by making a move that might not have been reciprocated.

I knocked on the doorframe to the kitchen, and she whipped around to face me. A grin crossed her face.

"Where were you?" I asked. "I got home a little bit ago, and I thought you were asleep."

"Heyyyyyyyyy," she said, the word drawn-out long and the tone sloppy.

Oh, Lord. She was drunk.

"Hey," I said, laughing. "You and Queen having a good time here all by yourselves? I leave you unattended for less than two days and you turn the apartment into a rave?"

She took a step toward me, and I glanced into the mixing bowl. She was still stirring some sort of batter, but at least it looked like she had actually followed some sort of recipe and wasn't just tossing in anything she could get her hands on.

"I was in my room," she said with a slight slur. "I splashed a lot of water on myself, and so I decided to change. Maybe I could have just taken my shirt off and baked topless. That," she said emphatically, flipping her spoon to underline the word and flinging a bit of batter in the process, "would be a popular cooking show."

The longer I looked at her, the more I noticed her face didn't look exactly right. It was a little puffy, and her eyes were red. It looked like she had tried to put makeup on, but a lot of it had just melted off again. She had been crying. I knew something was wrong.

"What happened?" I asked. Tears welled up in her eyes again, and her chin started to wobble. "Okay, let me just take this from you."

I grabbed onto the glass mixing bowl, but she latched on tighter, clinging it to her chest. I tugged on it again, finally managing to wrestle it free from her grasp. I'd dunked my finger in it during the scuffle, and I licked the batter off. It was loose, but it tasted like sugar cookies.

"Okay, let's try again. What happened?" I asked.

"Marshall is a pile of sweaty ball sacks is what happened," she said, her voice getting louder and higher. "And so is Ashley!"

She grabbed the bowl again, and we ended up in a brief tug-of-war. The bowl slipped from our hands, flipped upside down, and landed on the floor. She immediately burst into tears, and I wrapped an arm around her.

"It's alright," I said. "Don't worry about it. Everything's okay. Come on. Let's go into the living room for a minute."

I turned off the music and bundled Maya in my arms to help her into the living room. I sat her down and perched close beside her. She clung to me and cried hard for a few seconds. When it seemed like she was done with the worst of the breakdown, she lifted her head from my shoulder and looked at me.

"I'm a mess," she said. "And I think I'm a little drunk."

I nodded, moving hair away from her face. "I think so, too."

"That I'm a mess, or that I'm drunk?" she asked.

I considered my answer carefully for a few seconds. "Both."

She should have laughed, but instead she just gave a resigned nod and looked down at her hands where they were folded between her knees.

"Yeah."

"Alright, why don't you tell me why Marshall is a big pile of sweaty ball sacks?" I asked. "And Ashley. Is this Ashley Pride?"

"Yes," Maya said venomously. "Ashley Pride-in-herself-for-being-a-slut."

It came out like she was positive. It was both witty and scathing, so I went with it. Rubbing her back, I nodded.

"So, would it be safe for me to wager a guess that Ashley and Marshall are seeing each other now?" I asked.

"Seeing each other all over the place," Maya said. "Including in the apartment that I just moved out of. Correction, that I was just kicked out of."

"She moved in with him?" I asked.

"Yes," she said. "Today. Can you believe that? There's probably still food in the refrigerator that I bought, and there's already another woman living in the apartment."

"How did you find out?" I asked.

"I was having so much fun baking and I took a bubble bath, and everything seemed great, so I went on social media," she said.

"And you saw a picture?"

"It's just that I hadn't checked anything at all since I moved out. Nothing. So, I decided I would go on and just kind of poke around a little bit and catch up on what was going on in Shelby. Maybe while I was in there, I could unfriend him and make sure I didn't have to deal with seeing his stupid face anymore. But as soon as I opened it up, there it was," she said.

"That bad, eh?" I asked.

"They're all over each other, standing in front of his apartment. The apartment I lived in. Granted, I only lived there for three weeks, but still. I lived there."

"I'm sorry," I said.

"But it was like none of that even mattered. The two of them were standing there in front of the building, sucking face and holding the keys. And then the caption. It just said, 'moving day.' That's it. 'Moving day.' With an exclamation point, mind you. They were all excited to spread it out to the world. Do you think I got an exclamation point when I moved in?"

"I'm going to go out on a limb here and say no," I said.

"No," Maya said firmly. "I didn't. I didn't even get a caption. I didn't even get a picture to put a caption on. I just moved in, but she gets a whole damn celebration." She suddenly sagged forward, dropping her face into her hands. "I'm such an idiot. He was cheating on me. There I was, trying to make the apartment perfect for the two of us and thinking things were going so well between us, and he was sleeping with somebody I considered a friend."

I didn't know what to say to her. All I could do was scoop Maya up and help her to bed, then go into the kitchen and start cleaning up the aftermath of her culinary therapy. I swore to myself if I ever saw Marshall again, I was going to kill him.

MAYA

I didn't so much wake up on Sunday morning as get ejected out of sleep by my head pounding so hard, I could probably do a fairly convincing *Stomp* revival to the cadence. My eyes felt like the lids had taken on a sandpaper lining and my mouth was dry as a bone.

I wanted to just keep my eyes closed and bury myself in sleep again. But that wasn't an option. I was fairly certain my head might actually explode if I didn't take something soon.

I needed to drag myself out of bed with whatever tiny bit of energy I could possibly muster and go on a noble hunt for aspirin. And probably some water. The longer I was awake, the more aware I became of my sticky, sour mouth and tight, dry throat.

Sitting up did not improve matters at all. It only made my already suffering head swirl around and brought my awareness to the rest of my body aching. What the hell was wrong with me?

Then it hit me. Oh yeah. I had been drunk since Thursday. Considering it was now sometime Saturday morning or possibly early afternoon, I very well might have pickled myself. This was definitely not the best idea. I was far from a hard drinker, and I could probably count on one hand the number of times in my life I had been truly hangover-inducing drunk. This time, however, might count for at least three fingers.

This was not good planning. I should have stopped well before I got to my fourth batch of cupcakes. I thought the three beers I drank the other day at Lindsey's bar was a misdirected choice. This blew that right out of the water. All I wanted to do was fall over backward, roll up in my blankets like a burrito, and pray for either death or Monday.

Just thinking about my ex-asshole-boyfriend and ex-friend had gotten me so mad I finally decided to drink him out of my system. It felt like a good plan at the time. Blasting music and working my way through my recipe list, I felt like the basis for the next big breakup anthem. But this was where it got me now.

It took a few minutes to finally get myself on my feet and feel like I was stable enough to walk into the bathroom. I turned on the shower and while the water was warming, I searched through the medicine cabinet for a pain reliever. Brazenly going against the label's recommendation, I poured four of the tablets into my palm and popped them in my mouth.

Though I had been impressed by Greg's apartment not seeming completely like it was inhabited only by a bachelor, it was in that moment when I realized he still had room for growth. Starting with including cups in the bathroom. Without even a masculine polka-dotted or plaid Dixie in sight, I resorted to filling my cupped hands with water from the faucet and drank it down.

It perked me up just enough for me to be able to take

my clothes off and climb into the shower. I stood there hoping for reconstitution and a clearer mind. The painkiller was just starting to kick in and take the worst of the edge off the throbbing headache when I figured I couldn't stay in there any longer.

I got out, put on the most comfortable clothes I could without just straight-up getting back in pajamas, and went to face the music. Somewhere in the back of my mind, I vaguely remembered Greg coming home the night before. But honestly, my memories were still floating around somewhere in a vat of vodka.

I followed the smell of something cooking and made it to the kitchen. Leaned against the doorframe, I watched Greg make scrambled eggs and a stack of French toast. It took him a few seconds to notice I was there, but when he did, he gave me a grin.

"Morning, drunky. I figured I could return the favor and make you some breakfast. Come eat. You're going to want to get over the worst of this quickly. We've got places to go," he said.

I groaned a little. "I don't want to go anywhere."

"Too bad," he said without pity.

There was no point in arguing. And not just because I felt like I had temporarily lost touch with the majority of my grasp on vocabulary. I also knew Greg well enough to know he wasn't going to just accept me saying no and move on. If he had a plan, that was what was going to happen. Even if he had to toss me over his shoulder and bring me along with him.

Since I was really not feeling being brought out in public in the particular ensemble I had going for me right at that moment, it would be in my best interest to agree.

He brought me my breakfast, and I sat at the table shoveling in the savory scrambled eggs.

"These are really good," I said. "Are they different?"

"Bacon fat," Greg said.

My eyes slid over to him. "What?"

"Bacon fat," he repeated. "I put bacon fat in the pan rather than butter or cooking oil. It will help with the hangover. So will the French toast. And if all else fails, I made extra coffee."

I had already finished my first two cups, so I scooted the empty mug over to him, and Greg laughed. He went to fill it and came back with a piece of French toast for himself in his hand.

"So, where are we going?" I asked.

"We have a few errands to run. Things to help you get settled in here and make it your home," he said.

I was curious, and that helped me push through the lingering discomfort to finish eating, get dressed, and plaster on a bit of makeup so I could at least look halfway awake and functional. Greg grabbed his keys, and we got in his truck.

I tried to pay attention to where we were driving, seeing if I could recognize anything from my tour of Charlotte the other day. Nothing looked familiar, and after a short drive, we ended up in the parking lot of a furniture store.

"I like your living room furniture," I told him. "Why are you replacing it?"

"I'm not going to," Greg said, taking the keys out of the ignition and releasing his seat belts. "We are here for you."

"What do you mean?" I asked.

"You can't keep sleeping on the couch," he said. "As

well as you fit all curled up on it, eventually it's going to catch up with you. So, we are here for a bed."

"I can't afford a bed right now," I said. "Give me a few weeks to work, and then we'll talk. Until then, the couch is fine."

"This place has a really good payment plan policy, and I'm going to put the down payment down for you," he said.

"No," I said, shaking my head. "I'm not going to let you do that."

"Why not?" he asked. "I got a really nice check and a couple of bonuses for coming in second at the race. I want to do this for you. Besides, I should be an adult now and actually have a bed in my second bedroom."

We were back in that place where there was no point in me trying to talk him out of something. We would either sit out here in the parking lot and bicker until he gave up and went inside to pick it out for me, or I was going to go in and decide on my bed.

I was immensely grateful to Greg as soon as I picked out the bed and he put the down payment on it. But even more so that night when I put fresh sheets we had bought at our next stop on the new mattress and crawled in. Just for fun, I stretched my arms and legs out to their furthest extent, then flopped over onto my stomach and did it the other way.

The next morning, we were back into the rhythm of me making breakfast. I wouldn't go as far as to say I was completely feeling better, but it was enough for me to ignore for the most part. Greg came in with a smile and dropped a kiss to the top of my head. He had been doing that for as long as I could remember. That gesture went through phases for me. Sometimes it felt brotherly. Other times it spoke to the importance of our close friendship. And sometimes it felt like something else.

I didn't let myself think about those times.

"How did you sleep?" he asked.

"Like a rock," I said. "Maybe even better than a rock, because I had a pillow."

"You know, rock sleep disparity is truly the great social injustice of our time. More awareness needs to be brought to it," Greg said as he poured his coffee.

"I'm considering an organization," I said.

That morning I felt in the mood for oatmeal, and I had a row of bowls filled with various mix-ins down the center of the dining table. Setting the massive pot of fresh oatmeal on a trivet in the middle of the table, I added two bowls and spoons at our settings. Greg brought in orange juice and glasses, and we sat down for breakfast.

"What are you going to bring to the barbecue tonight?" he asked while dumping half the bowl of raisins into his oatmeal.

I paused with my spoon still in the brown sugar. "What barbecue tonight?"

"The weekly Freeman Sunday get-together," he said as if I should automatically know what the hell he was talking about and why I had anything to do with it.

"I ask again, what barbecue tonight?"

"I told you they get together every week for dinner either at Minnie and Gus's house, or Quentin's house. This week it's at Quentin's house," Greg said.

"You didn't tell me I would be going to it," I said.

"Absolutely. Merry called this morning to make sure I was bringing you. She wants you to bring something," he said.

"Really?"

"Yeah," he said, nodding and giving me an incredulous

look. "They really like you, Maya. They want you to be a part of the group."

I didn't know what to say and the emotion of it started to tighten in my throat and make me feel a little thrown off. Not wanting to show it, I shook off the feeling and detoured the conversation.

"What should I bring?" I asked.

Greg glanced back toward the kitchen. "I vote some of these baked goods. Let's share the wealth."

I laughed and agreed. At least the overpopulation of the kitchen caused by my temporary breakdown had a silver lining.

I was feeling mostly human by the time we got to Quentin's house that evening. I was stunned when we drove up into the driveway and I saw the sprawling mansion.

"Wow," I said. "This place is amazing."

"Yeah," Greg said. "You would never know they were all multimillionaires, would you?" He paused like he was contemplating that thought. "I think Quentin and Vince might actually be billionaires. Nick is getting close. Darren is much younger than them, so he still has time, but even he's way up there."

I sat in the car and stared, openmouthed. "Seriously?" Greg nodded, and I shook my head. "They don't seem like it."

"Nope. Part of why I like them as much as I do."

We got out of the truck, and Greg helped me carry the two boxes of cookies, cupcakes, and bread along with my favorite pasta salad and the cream cheese, olives, and green pepper pinwheels I brought to every party. I felt almost embarrassed by them now. It just didn't feel right carrying a platter of flour tortillas spread with cream cheese, ranch dressing mix, cheese, and chopped-up vegetables into a house that looked like this.

But I shouldn't have worried about it. There wasn't a single judgmental look, and Darren's best friend, Colby, ended up eating at least half of the platter while we waited for dinner. I was immediately swamped by people wanting to see what goodies I brought and giving me hugs.

A couple of the guys gave me offers to dismember Marshall, and I told them I would tuck that away in my back pocket for if the mood struck me. Being there warmed me up inside, and by the time we were sitting around eating grilled steaks on the back porch, I didn't feel so angry anymore.

I was starting to think Marshall had done me a favor.

12

GREG

"That was really fun," Maya said as we drove back to my apartment after dinner at Quentin's house.

"Yeah, Quentin and Merry know how to do a gathering. He was always pretty good at entertaining, but since he aligned himself with Merry, it's been a whole new level. She fancies herself a social media expert, but what she really should be is a party planner. Maybe a wedding coordinator," I said.

"I bet their wedding was gorgeous," she said with a hint of a sigh in her voice.

I laughed. "Actually, she was eight months pregnant, wearing jean shorts and a white sleeveless top, and they did it right out in the middle of the field on the compound. Honestly, that was perfect for them at that point. She just wanted to be married before the baby was here, and that field was really important in their relationship. It's still one of their favorite places."

"You know," Maya said, nodding, "I could totally see that. And yet, I bet she pulled it off."

"She did, actually. She managed to make cutoff jean shorts and a white tank top bridal," I said.

Maya laughed. "Thank you for bringing me out there. I was really nervous about going, but it was nice. I really like all of them. You know how weird that is? To actually be around that many people and not have a single one of them that you want to avoid talking to?"

"They have that effect," I said. "But don't let them fool you. They aren't always nice when anyone offends or hurts the people they love."

"So, I guess you fit in with them in that way, too," she said.

I felt warmth in the middle of my chest when she said that. It was exactly what I was hoping she would think of me. I wanted her to know I would always protect her, always take care of her. No matter how long we were apart, or what went into that separation, I didn't want her to ever question that she was safe with me.

"Speaking of being nervous, though, how are you feeling about work starting up tomorrow?" I asked, trying to gloss over the tense emotion that suddenly started building up between us. "Lindsey was talking about it while we were getting food. She's looking forward to having you around. She feels bad it's nothing fancier."

"Definitely shouldn't feel bad," Maya said. "She's a complete lifesaver. After all this time, I still haven't heard from either one of those little shops that I applied to. If Lindsey hadn't given me this job, I wouldn't have anything, and I would have no idea what I was going to do next."

"And I can assure you Lindsey is a great person. I know you've only interacted with her a couple of times, but she's awesome. She's funny and caring. She'll take really good care of you," I said.

"I know she will," Maya said. "And I'm determined to prove myself to her and move up as much as I possibly can whenever she has another position for me. I'm really looking forward to spending more time with her. I really like her so far, and it's also nice to have another connection to the same group."

I nodded. "As a matter of fact, after races, we usually end up at the bar celebrating. It's home base when we aren't at the compound."

"So, what you're actually telling me is that you're going to have plenty of opportunity to come to the bar and make fun of me while I'm working in the kitchen," Maya said.

"Maybe," I replied. "Is she going to make you wear a hairnet while you're working on the line?"

"I would think so," she said.

"Then, yes, definitely. I'll be there," I said.

Maya laughed and shook her head. "Perfect."

The next morning, I was feeling guilty for not being able to be there with Maya when she left for her first day of work.

Unfortunately, her hours at the bar took up the afternoon and into the night, overlapping with my hours at the compound by several. That meant she would be getting ready and heading out when I was already at work, then getting home well after me. I wanted to make sure she still felt like I was thinking about her and sending her all the best, so while she was showering Monday morning, I packed her lunch.

I made her favorite sandwich from when we were kids and stuffed in a few of the special treats and snacks I'd bought when she didn't notice. It was far from the healthiest options and definitely didn't look like an adult's lunch, but hopefully she would get the sentiment and it would make her feel good.

I added a note telling her I hoped she had a good day and that I was proud of her, tucked it into the refrigerator along with the lunch, then went back to my normal morning. It was possibly a bit more domestic than was strictly necessary or appropriate between roommates, but there was no way I could talk myself out of it. I kept finding myself drawn to the box of candy-speckled brownies.

At least I wouldn't be there when she found it.

We ate breakfast, and I gave her a hug before heading out to the compound. Like usual, I was there first, and I spent some time going over the stats from the last race so I could set my sights on improving my performance. Darren arrived a little later, and we went to work making modifications and improvements to our bikes.

I was working on building and customizing a second racing bike to try out later in the season. There were some modifications and features I wanted to try, but I didn't want to completely change the bike I had been using. I could compare the performance of both machines and determine which was best for each individual race.

In the middle of the afternoon, I heard my phone alert me to a new text message. I wiped my hands off on a cloth as I crossed the garage to where I had my phone sitting on the work counter.

The message was from Maya. A sandwich emoji followed by a big smile and a hug told me she found her lunch. After that, a stream of disconnected, unrelated emojis told me she had only recently discovered the full extent of her emoji options and wanted to try them out. The last one was a small pile of smiling poop, followed by a long string of question marks.

I laughed and immediately felt a hard poke in the middle of my back. I turned around to find Gus standing behind me, eyeing me suspiciously.

"Interesting message?" he asked.

"No," I said.

"Mmmm-hmmmm," the older man replied, turning back to his work on the custom bike he was building.

"What's going on?" Kelly asked as she and Darren came back into the garage from going on a snack break.

"Nothing," I said.

Kelly paused, and her eyes slid over to Gus, who just shook his head at her. I set my phone down and pushed the interaction out of my mind so I could focus on the work in front of me.

That evening, I had forgotten that Maya wasn't going to be at the apartments when I got home from work. I walked in expecting to find her lounging in the living room or baking to the '80s. Instead, I opened the door and stepped into silence.

It was weird for the apartment to be empty. After living alone for five years here in Charlotte, it would seem that I would be used to my apartment being quiet when I got home. Instead, it felt almost eerie. I had gotten used to her presence and very much noticed her not being there.

I went into my bedroom to drop my stuff and change out of my work clothes. The door to her bedroom was standing partially open, and I peeked in. She had set up her new bed and made it with the bedding set we'd bought after leaving the furniture store. The couch was now shoved up against the wall on the other side of the room, and she had added throw pillows that were originally intended for the bed.

It was good to see the room looking like her more and

more. It was no longer just a spare bedroom or somewhere she was crashing. It was really Maya's now, and I looked forward to seeing all the other ways she would personalize it as she settled in more.

Seeing the room and breathing in the smell of her there made me miss her. Not that I was about to admit that to anyone. And especially not to her. I considered going to the bar to see her and check in on how she was doing but I stopped myself before I headed out of the apartment. I didn't want to bother her on her first day or make her feel like I didn't believe in her. Or, even worse, like she was in a fishbowl and I was going to be monitoring her every movement.

She was already nervous enough and wanted to prove herself. Having me there as a chaperone wouldn't do her any good. I wanted her to feel comfortable and at home in Charlotte, and that included at work. I would hear all about it when she got home.

Putting aside the idea of going out, I opened the refrigerator to find something to eat. As soon as I looked inside, I laughed. Whether it was sarcastic payback or a nice gesture to mark the first day of us figuring out our staggered schedules, the salad decked out in a pink Post-it note with a large heart would be my dinner.

I took it out, grabbed a bottle of water to go along with it, and headed into the living room. As long as I was alone in the apartment for the evening, I might as well catch up on my guilty pleasure. Maya didn't yet know about my investment in *The Voice*, so I was behind by a couple of episodes.

I sat down on the couch and settled in for a binge. I took a couple bites of the field greens, grilled chicken, and vinaigrette and turned on the TV.

1 3

MAYA

I didn't really know what to expect when I went into the bar. Lindsey called me before I showed up and told me to go in through the back. It was a strange experience. It felt both like I was being shuffled around so I would stay out of sight, and like I was being given some sort of special access.

I decided to focus on the special feeling. After all, what I'd told Greg was true. I was extremely lucky Lindsey even gave me this position. I wasn't going to care what it was. It would be ridiculous to think that working in the kitchen of a bar was beneath me. It was real, honest work, and something that needed to be done.

The skillset wasn't necessarily the same as what I'd used in my previous job, but that didn't matter. I was a quick learner and would happily put as much effort and attention into anything Lindsey asked me to do as I possibly could. Not just because I wanted to climb the ladder and get to a higher position at some point. But also, just because it was the right thing to do.

"Hey," Lindsey said when I walked in. "I'm glad you're

here. We actually just had somebody call out for the night, so this is a great time for you to be starting."

"You just tell me whatever you need me to do. I'm happy to jump in however I can," I said.

"Great to hear," she said. "Let me give you a tour. I know you've been here before, but I want to show you all the places you don't see when you're just a customer. First, let's go get you clocked in for your very first shift," she said.

It was ridiculous, considering I had used a very similar system to clock into every shift I worked at the Cabinet Factory, but getting my personal code and signing into the system to track my hours sent a little bit of a thrill through me.

Maybe it was because I knew I got this position for myself. Technically, I supposed Lindsey just handed it to me, but I didn't have a boyfriend or family member to thank for getting me the job. And this meant it was really mine, and that was exciting. It was small, but it was a first step.

After clocking in, Lindsey brought me back to the kitchen and showed me around. She introduced me to the couple of other staff members who had already arrived to start prepping for the evening.

"When I took over this place for my dad, I never would have thought that food was going to be so much focus of it. When he ran it, and my grandfather before him, it was definitely just a neighborhood bar. It had a kind of pub feeling where everybody was basically a regular and bartender could fill your drink just because you walked through the door," Lindsey said.

"That sounds nice, too," I said.

She nodded. "Oh, it definitely was. People love this place, and it's where I grew up. But when I took over, I just felt like I should make it my own. People would always ask for more food options, so I started adding a couple of things here and there. Eventually, the menu grew, and now we're actually a place people come on purpose to have dinner."

"You mentioned you were thinking about expanding to a restaurant," I said.

"That's the vision. I've started renting the entire thing out to people who want to have special events here. If I expand out to a restaurant, it will have even more space for things like that, and I can offer more food options, too. Maybe even breakfast and lunch. Possibly a boxed lunch or custom small-scale catering so people could order dinners to pick up and bring home."

It sounded like the idea excited her, and I looked forward to the possibility of being a part of seeing that dream coming true for her.

"How do you want me to get started?" I asked.

"Well, you can help the line cooks do some of the basic prep. Fill condiment and ingredient containers, unload the food deliveries that are sitting in the coolers. That sort of thing. Then we'll see from there. Welcome aboard," she said.

"Thank you," I said. "I really appreciate this."

"No problem. Let me know if you need anything," she said.

She left the kitchen, and I offered myself over to the line cook to get started. The rest of my first shift was a success. It was busy and tiring, but that's exactly how I expected it to be. It was how I wanted it to be. I played busboy, keeping the tables turning over as fast as possible to accommodate all the people who wanted to come in. After cleaning off the tables, I helped with washing dishes.

I even had a chance to be a back server and bring food out to a couple of tables when things got busy. I was constantly moving, constantly doing something with my eye on my next task. Lindsey watched me closely throughout the night. I noticed her nod every time I took on a new task or did something right.

The validation felt good. I liked that I was doing well and proving to her that I could not only be an asset, but that I took the position she gave me seriously.

I kept working until the bar closed and the last customer left. It was just after two in the morning when I finally took a breath and dropped down onto one of the stools at the bar. The servers came up, and I was surprised to see them empty out the pockets of their aprons onto the bar. The bartender did the same, and Lindsey emptied her own pockets into the pile.

"Good tippers tonight," a waitress named Daisy said.

"Looks like it," Lindsey said, scooping all the money together before counting it up.

She jotted down the total amount on a small notebook she kept in her pocket, then started dividing it up into several small piles. I didn't realize what she was doing until she offered one of them to me.

"What's this?" I asked.

"Tips for the night," she said.

"But those belong to the servers and bartenders," I said.

"We pool," Daisy said. "Everybody here works hard. We shouldn't be the only ones who get tips. At the end of the night, we add up everything we got and divide it up. Trust me, you deserve it. You were hopping all night. We appreciate what you do. Because you work as hard as you do, it lets us serve more customers, which gets us more tips. So, you deserve some of it."

I looked at Lindsey, who gave me a slight smile and nod. "Thanks."

I went home that night with more than $75 in tips and hoarding all the smiles I got from my new boss and coworkers.

By the time I got back to the apartment, it was quiet and dark. I realized Greg was in bed and felt a flicker of sadness. The only downside to having this new job was that I was hardly ever going to be able to see him. Just like Lindsey said, the hours did kind of suck. I worked almost eleven hours that day, and she had mentioned that was not uncommon. I was scheduled for specific days and start times, but not end times.

It was the unspoken expectation that I would keep working as long as I was needed each night. Sometimes that wouldn't be as late because the night wasn't as busy or there would be more staff members there. Other nights I would be there past closing to help wrap things up.

I was fine with that. Every hour worked meant more money in my pocket and building more of my reputation. But it also meant I would come home from work when Greg was still sleeping, and he would go to work in the morning when I was in bed. We would only see each other on days off.

I got Thursday night as my official day off, and Sunday when the bar was closed. Greg technically got the weekends off unless there was a race, but he had already told me it wasn't an infrequent event for him to work through the weekend just as much as he did on the weekdays. It created somewhat of a lonely feeling in me, but at least I was there in the apartment. And at least I was in Charlotte.

One of the perks of working at the bar was getting to bring home food at the end of the night. After running around so much, the sandwich and snacks Greg left for me seemed very far away, and I was starving by the time I dropped down onto the couch in the living room to eat.

The chicken and dumplings I chose was delicious. Relaxing on the couch watching throwback TV shows while eating it straight out of the to-go container was strangely luxurious.

I went to bed that night thinking about the money I'd rolled up into a sock and shoved in the top drawer of the dresser that came along with the bed in my bedroom set. For now, this would suffice for stashing tips, but I would need to start a bank account for my paychecks. With that added to my mental to-do list, I fell asleep.

The sun was already high in the sky when I woke up the next morning. I padded into the kitchen to find something to eat and discovered another lunch packed for me in the refrigerator. It made me giggle, and I pulled out the ingredients to make a pan of pasta. It would be perfect for eating before work.

It seemed like we were getting into the habit of leaving each other food every day, so I decided to lean into it. It was a nice way to continue to acknowledge each other even when we weren't able to see one another. And every time he did something like that, it was a reminder of just how long it had been since I really felt like anybody took care of me.

It felt good to be cared for. Even if it was just by my best friend whose life I pretty much crashed. But I figured there was nobody else I wanted taking care of me more.

When the pasta was done and cooled, I put some on a plate with a foil-wrapped piece of garlic bread and a salad in a bowl beside it. I took the pink sticky notes I'd bought out of the junk drawer and made another heart, then stuck it to the plastic over the plate.

Grabbing the lunch he packed for me, I headed to the bar, feeling oddly at peace.

14

GREG

I found myself looking forward to Thursday all week. I knew that was her night off, which meant we might actually get a chance to see each other. I hadn't even laid eyes on her awake since Monday when I left for work, and the days were stretching out long.

On Thursday morning, I woke up at my usual time to get ready to go to work. She was still sleeping after not getting home from the bar until hours after I had gone to bed. I happened to wake up with the sound of her rummaging around in the kitchen and noticed it was almost 3:30 in the morning before dropping back to sleep, which meant she would probably stay in bed for a good while after I left for the compound.

I knew she wasn't going into work that day, but it didn't stop me from putting together lunch for her. We had already established the rhythm, and I wasn't going to break it, even if she didn't have to go into the bar.

It was even more important for me to spend extra time with Maya that day. On top of not seeing her for three days at that point, I would also be gone most of the weekend and might not get a chance to spend much time with her then.

There was another race on Saturday, this time during the day rather than the evening, which means I would be heading out even earlier that morning. Depending on the turnout, we might end up at Lindsey's that night, but that didn't mean she was going to get to come out and hang out with us.

The only other night of the week she got off was Sunday, but considering we would both be exhausted, it was entirely possible we'd end up sleeping the majority of the day. Then I would need to head to the compound to get everything broken down after the race.

I was different than the other guys in that way. It was tradition to close down the compound the day after a successful race, and the family never went in on Sunday. But I hated going into the garage on Monday and finding lingering work from the week before. I'd rather start my week with as much of a clean slate as possible, which meant having to unload the equipment and at least clean my bike.

Maybe I could convince Maya to come with me and hang out while I did all those things. I would probably feel guilty even asking her. After a long week of work, the last thing she probably wanted to do was sit around and watch me clean and repair a motorcycle.

The day seemed especially long, even though I left well before I usually did. I got back to the apartment and found Maya in the kitchen cooking dinner. There was already a Post-it note with a heart on it stuck to the dining room table where I usually sat.

It was one of those things I wanted to mention, but at the same time I felt like I shouldn't. Like it was an unspoken secret that carried meaning we were supposed to feel but not discuss.

"Something smells good," I said instead.

She looked over her shoulder at me and smiled. "Thank you. It's amazing how much more elaborate a meal I can make when I actually have the entire evening to do it. I'm making pot roast tonight."

"Sounds amazing. It's been years since I've had pot roast," I said. "What about for dessert? Would I be getting too nostalgic to hope for apple pie?"

My last food memory of having pot roast with Maya was when her mother had made it for us when we were small children. I didn't remember why I was at her house having dinner, or if there was any specific occasion that inspired the pot roast and pie, but it was a good memory. Maya didn't seem to feel the same way. She shook her head emphatically.

"Absolutely not," she said. "There will be no pie. I still haven't come to the point where I'm ready to be friendly with pie."

"Fair enough," I said.

"But I did make homemade pudding," she said.

"Chocolate or vanilla?" I asked.

"Butterscotch," she answered.

"The very best answer," I said. I kissed her on the top of the head. "Alright, I'm going to go take a really quick shower because I got super grimy at work. I'll be back in just a minute to help you in any way I can."

"Nothing for you to do," she said. "But I will be ready to dig into this when you're done."

I took a shower, and by the time I got out, she had already set the table and was serving up huge portions of the tender meat and delicious vegetables. She seemed to remember the carrots were my favorite part because she added a few extras to my plate before putting it at my spot.

We sat down and talked about work and our lives over the last three days while we ate. When we were done, I helped her clear the table.

"Are you ready for dessert?" she asked.

"Not quite yet," I said. "But I had an idea."

"What?" she asked.

"Why don't we do all of these dishes, then go downstairs and take a swim."

"A swim?"

"Yeah," I said. "There's a huge, beautiful pool at the clubhouse. You haven't even been in it. It's still hot out, so why don't we go take a dip? The pool is open twenty-four hours a day, but nobody ever goes there in the dark. It would just be the two of us."

She thought about it for a few seconds, then nodded.

"Okay, that actually sounds like fun." she said.

We finished cleaning up the kitchen and putting away all the leftovers, then went into our bedrooms to change into bathing suits. I realized then that I hadn't even asked Maya if she had a bathing suit. I just assumed she did because she had what I figured was everything she owned with her.

Sure enough, a couple minutes later, she walked out into the living room in a pair of shorts and an open button-up shirt over a simple black bathing suit. Her flip-flops showed off that her toenails were painted bright, glossy red, and for some reason that made me smile. I grabbed a couple of towels out of the linen closet and tossed one over to her.

"Additional bonus for swimming at night rather than during the day, we don't have to put on sunscreen," I said.

"How edgy of you," she said, flipping the towel over her

shoulder and walking over to the door with an overexaggerated swing of her hips.

I laughed and followed her. We walked along the sidewalk to the pool, and I used the key card issued to all tenants to open the lock.

"I need to talk to the landlord about getting one of these to you as soon as possible," I said. "You have to use it to access the pool and the clubhouse, and to get your mail."

She kicked off her flip-flops and slipped the shirt back off her shoulders to put it on her chair. I tried hard not to ogle her when she took off her shorts and stood in front of me in only her bathing suit. She looked incredible. There was no need for an overtly sexy suit or even a two-piece. The simple black one-piece accentuated all of her curves and was unapologetically sultry.

She walked over to the pool and dipped her toe into the sparkling water.

"How is it?" I asked.

"Chilly," she said. "But it feels good."

Rather than walking down the steps, she walked a few feet down the edge of the pool and dove in. I laughed as she surfaced.

"There's the girl I remember," I said. "No fear. No hesitation."

"Do things before I think them all the way through?" she asked.

"Maybe sometimes," I said. "But it's good. People miss out on the best things in life because they think about it too much."

"How about you?" she asked. "Are you going to think too much?"

The question had an unexpected effect on me. I forced myself to push away the reaction and took off running toward the edge of the pool. She screamed as my cannonball sent up a huge splash and a wave that nearly knocked her over.

For the next hour, we swam and splashed, laughing and sliding through the water together. She got closer to me, and a few times I reached out just to brush the tips of my fingers against her to make sure she was really there. I thought I was doing a great job at not drooling over her, but my dedication to a purely friendly swim disappeared with the appearance of a group of guys I recognized from the first floor of our building.

They walked through the gate with their eyes already locked on Maya. A couple of them made kissy sounds toward her, and I heard a few inappropriate comments they probably thought were muttered under their breaths. Or maybe they didn't.

These guys struck me as the type who would think she should be flattered to hear them talking about her like that.

She wasn't.

I didn't say anything. I didn't try to lay claim, even though that was what was boiling in my veins. It wasn't my place to be jealous, but at the same time, I could see Maya's discomfort when she looked over at me. My protectiveness surged up, and I got closer to her in the water.

All that did was start them up with a whole new set of comments. Finally, Maya moved to the edge of the pool and started to get out. I positioned myself so they wouldn't be able to look at her ass as she pulled herself up, then got out and followed her over to the chairs. She grabbed one of the towels and wrapped it around herself, and I sat down at the edge of the seat.

As the guys kept talking, it seemed like Maya had enough. She dropped down to sit in my lap, wrapping her arms around my neck and nuzzling into it. I knew exactly what she was doing, but that didn't stop my heart and body from responding. This was a serious problem.

Fortunately, the guys got the picture and made their way out of the pool area. As soon as they were out of sight, Maya jumped up. I was glad she moved quick, otherwise the situation could have gotten very uncomfortable, very fast.

We didn't stay at the pool much longer. The group of guys had marred our simple fun, and neither of us felt like lingering around there any longer. We went back to the apartment, and she immediately got in the shower. I waited for her to get out and come talk to me, but she slipped into her bedroom and closed the door.

I took a shower and got into bed but couldn't fall asleep. I stared at the ceiling, thinking about the way I reacted to her at the pool, which was something I couldn't let happen. Before closing my eyes to go to sleep, I promised myself I was going to get over it.

15

MAYA

For the second Saturday in a row, I woke up to an uncomfortable sensation. This week, it was my phone vibrating against the side of my head. Not quite as miserable and painful as my hangover the week before, but not fun, nonetheless.

I had forgotten that I turned the ringer off before going to bed and had apparently fallen asleep while watching TV on the tiny screen. At some point during the night, it ended up being shoved under my pillow, which meant when the phone call came in while I was still deep in sleep, it jiggled against my skull like a tiny jackhammer.

Dredging myself up into reluctant consciousness, I snatched the phone up and looked at the screen. My stomach sank when I saw it was Lindsey. Could I have possibly slept that late? I knew I was exhausted and wanted to get a little bit of extra rest on Saturday before the busy end of the week crowds came in, but I didn't think I possibly could have slept long enough to be late to work.

"I'm so sorry," I said by way of answering the phone. "I'm on my way."

"Maya?" Lindsey asked. "Where are you on your way to? Why are you sorry?"

"Work because I'm late?"

She laughed. "I'm the one who's sorry. You must have been asleep."

"A little bit," I said.

"Well, you didn't oversleep. It's only 9:30 in the morning. You most definitely are not late for work. And there's no way you're going to be late for work today, because we're not going into the bar today," she said.

I sat in confused silence for a few seconds. "We're not?"

"No," she said. "That's why I'm calling you. I wanted to invite you to go see the guys ride today. The race is local, so we can drive over there together and watch them. What do you think?"

I was still somewhat hesitant to watch Greg, but I figured I couldn't actually avoid it forever. There was going to come a time when I was going to run out of excuses, and it would just seem rude that I didn't come to a race. I remembered what Greg had said when I dove into the pool. No fear, no hesitation.

"Sure, that sounds like a lot of fun. I'll pick you up. That way I can drive Greg back home rather than somebody having to bring him all the way to the complex to pick up his car."

"Great," Lindsey said. "I'll see you in about an hour?"

"Sure. Text me your address so I can put it in the GPS. And don't tell anybody I'm coming. I don't want Greg to know. I want it to be a surprise," I said.

"No problem," she said with a hint of something in her voice.

Without acknowledging that something, I got off the phone and got out of bed.

I didn't have much time, so after getting dressed, I was rushing to get to Lindsey's house. Another massive home greeted me, and I realized she must live with Vince already. His house was distinctly different than his brother Quentin's, but no less impressive.

Lindsey wasn't waiting outside, so I took out my phone and called her to let her know I was there. She sounded rushed and a little bit frazzled when she answered. She apologized several times and promised she would be right out. I felt better for being in so much of a hurry and cutting it close getting to her house.

A few minutes after I arrived, the door opened, and Lindsey stepped out with a little boy. She held tight to his hand as she locked the door, then gently guided him over to the side of the stairs leading down from the porch and wrapped his hand around the handrail. She took hold of the other hand, and they slowly made their way down the steps. I noticed she was talking to him as they went, but his head didn't move to look at her.

That was when I realized her son was blind. It wasn't something that she or anyone else had mentioned to me when talking about him. He was just Remy, the almost four-year-old boy with too much personality for his tiny size, who was going to give the world a run for its money when he grew up.

Watching him get down to the bottom of the steps and skip happily along the sidewalk made my heart swell. I loved that they didn't mention his disability. It just wasn't something that they figured defined him, and it obviously didn't. Lindsey was careful and cautious with him, just as any parent would be with a young child going down steep brick steps. But the little boy seemed unfazed and just eager to keep going.

When they were close to the car, Lindsey smiled at me and waved. She held up a finger to ask me to wait, then walked over to her car. She said something to Remy, and he put one hand on the car and stood still. By his shuffling little feet and bouncing, I could tell he didn't particularly like standing still. He wanted to be jumping and playing, but he did as his mother asked.

She reached into the car and pulled out a car seat. She brought it over to the truck and not for the first time since my father left it to me, I was thankful that he had chosen an extended cab that had a back seat.

She was able to fit the car seat into the middle of the back and secure it firmly in place. Remy scrambled up and sat down so she could secure his harness. When he was in place, she backed out of the car and climbed into the front seat. Letting out a sigh, she turned to me with a smile.

"Hi," she said.

I laughed. "Hi. How are you doing?"

"It's been one of those mornings," she said. "But we are very excited to be going to the race, aren't we, Remy?" The little boy let out a cheer and threw his arms up in the air. "Remy, this is Miss Maya. She's friends with Mr. Greg. Maya, this is my son, Remy. You didn't get to meet him at the dinner at Quentin's house because he was with his father that night."

"Hi, Remy. It's nice to meet you," I said.

"Hi, Miss Maya," he said. "I like Mr. Greg. He's nice."

I smiled into the rearview mirror even though I knew he couldn't see me. "I like Mr. Greg, too. We've been friends for a long time."

She gave me directions to the racetrack, and we got there just in time. We made our way to the stands, and she pointed down to the pit row. We were several rows up, but I was still able to clearly see Greg and the others from that vantage point. I watched him for a few moments. He stood with his hands on his hips, looking out over the track and occasionally turning to Darren at his side and saying something. Darren pointed to the other side, and both men nodded.

Greg must have sensed someone watching him, because he turned around and scanned the crowd. He spotted me, and his face lit up. I grinned and waved, my heart trembling slightly in my chest as I realized I couldn't remember anyone ever being that happy to see me.

Lindsey's elbow dug into my side, and I looked over at her. She grinned and made kissy faces at me. It was the embodiment of the note in her voice that I heard when she called to ask if I wanted to go to the race with her that day. I laughed and shook my head.

"It's not like that," I said.

"Are you sure? Greg was pretty damn happy to see you here."

"He didn't know I was coming," I said. "He did ask me to go to that first race, but I said no. So, he didn't think I was coming to this one. He's just happy that I'm here to see him ride. It's been a long time since we hung out, that's all."

"Sure. Have you ever seen him ride?" she asked.

"Yeah," I said. "I mean, obviously nothing like this. But he used to tinker around with bikes when we were back in Shelby. We were just kids, but he was still amazing at mechanical things like that. He could take a broken-down old bike that nobody had ridden in decades and turn it into something incredible. And when he was done, he always brought me out to this old, abandoned school and rode around.

She looked at me suspiciously. "But there was never anything between you? Nothing at all?"

"Nothing but friendship," I said. "We've always been just friends. He is the absolute best friend I have ever had. But that's it."

Even saying it brought a slight twist to my stomach. It made me think about the last couple of weeks that Greg lived in Shelby. We had graduated from high school and were trying to figure out life. Greg couldn't stand living at home anymore. His father was a drunk and was getting worse by the day. He hated seeing the way he treated his mother, but she wouldn't leave him.

In the middle of senior year, Greg had gotten into a brawl with his father. To protect him, his mother sent him off to live with his aunt. She was sweet, but he didn't want to be there, either. That was when he started talking about moving to Charlotte. He wanted me to go with him. He said we could have such an amazing life here.

But I didn't go. I told him I had gotten into college and was thinking about my future. It was just a small local college, not any sort of high-powered university or anything, but it was an achievement for me. I didn't want to just leave that behind, and I thought maybe he would change his mind. Or at least wait for a little while.

He showed up at my house drunk, talking about how I didn't need to go to college, that he would make sure I was okay. He would take care of me. I told him to stop. I didn't want to hear what I knew he was going to say. It had been building up in me for years, and I never made a move. I never said a single word or let on what I was feeling. I didn't want to hear it from him, either.

We couldn't do that. We couldn't cross that line. His friendship was far too precious to me for me to be willing to throw it away for something we didn't even know would work. So, I tried desperately to get him to stop talking. But he didn't. And that night, he admitted he thought about us being together. Maybe if we moved to Charlotte, he said. Maybe we could start something new.

I sent him away, telling him to sober up. When he did, he acted like he had never even said it. I never mentioned it again, and neither did he. To that day, I didn't know if he even remembered that conversation. A few weeks later, he was gone. We kept up with phone calls and emails, but far too soon, those petered out as we both got busy, and before I knew it, we had completely lost touch.

It was devastating, but I forced myself to put it aside. Maybe he and I had gotten from each other all we needed to —all we were supposed to. Now it was time for us to live our lives. Finding Marshall helped distract me. It reminded me of the types of relationships I should have been looking for. My friendship with Greg had kept me from finding a serious boyfriend. Now I had him.

Looking back, I was sad I ever let us grow apart. I was sad I did the exact thing he said I never did. I hesitated.

Shaking off the melancholy, I threw myself into the experience of the race. I was no longer afraid of watching him. I was excited to see him do his thing and absolutely crush it.

16

GREG

Soaring over that finish line with the rest of the riders behind me was a moment I would never forget. It wasn't the first time I'd won a race, but it definitely felt like it was. I was grinning so hard my face hurt, and I could barely control myself long enough to bring the bike to a safe stop before I wanted to jump off and leap into the air in celebration. I let out a cheer of excitement before I even took my helmet off. By the time I got it off and it was hanging from the handlebar of my bike, I could see the wall of people rushing toward me.

Darren got to me first. He'd come in second and was only a few feet away. We grab each other in a tight embrace, pounding each other's backs and congratulating one another in overlapping voices. Though we were in direct competition with each other, we were also friends and actually did want each other to succeed. Plus, a win for Freeman Racing was a win, no matter which of us brought it home.

There wasn't a single question in my mind that Darren never held back. He never let me win or cut me any slack so that I could boost my record. There would be no benefit to that. It would damage his own career, and if I found out about it, he knew I would be furious.

So, his excitement and happiness for my win was absolutely genuine. As was the same sentiment from the rest of the crew. We hugged and cheered, then headed for the official celebration area near the finish line. As I was walking toward it, Maya came running toward me. I opened up my arms, and she jumped into them. I swung her around as she laughed and squealed.

"You were amazing," she said. "Seriously, that was incredible to watch."

"Thank you," I said. "Come on, come with me."

"Where are you going?" she asked.

"To let people fawn on me and present me with my winnings," I said with dramatic flair. She laughed, and I reached for her hand. "Come on. I want you to come with me."

She took my hand and let me guide her through the crowd pressing in around us to the small platform erected next to the track. I helped her up onto it with me, and she stood close by my side as the race organizers handed me my check and trophy. I held the trophy up high above my head as photographers took pictures from every angle.

A couple of times, I glanced at Maya out of the corner of my eye. I wanted to make sure she was doing alright. She looked slightly overwhelmed, but not in a way that I worried about her. More just like she was trying to take it all in, absorb every single second so she could remember it.

If I had my way, this would be far from the last time she experienced any of this. Now that I had her by my side while I was celebrating a win, I never wanted to be without it. I wanted to have this moment over and over.

Somebody shook up a beer and held it so it sprayed right at me. Maya let out a squeal and curled into me, tucking her face against my chest. I wrapped my arm around her and held her close, laughing with her. A couple of reporters came up to ask questions and get the sound bites and bits of footage they would use in the news over the next couple of days.

When it was finally over, I turned to Maya. Gus had already taken the trophy and the large novelty version of the winnings check so he could bring them back to the compound. He liked to display the checks in the main building because he thought they were hilarious. The trophy would be set on a stand in the main lobby until the next race, then it would go home with me.

He'd started doing the rotation of the race trophies well before I started racing with the team. It was a chance to constantly show off the successes and accomplishments of the team without just having a massive trophy room where no one would ever see the awards.

I took both of Maya's hands and leaned close so she would be able to hear me talk over the continued shouting and music around us.

"You've got to come to the garage with me," I said.

"The garage?" she asked. "To drop off the equipment?"

"No. We're having a party," I said. It looked like she was still struggling to hear me, so I tugged on her hands to pull her over to a quieter area of the track. "I said we're having a party. Usually after a win at the local track, we go to Lindsey's bar to celebrate. But it's closed tonight."

"She closed the bar?" Maya asked. "I thought she just took the night off so that she could come to the race."

"She did," Greg said. "She was going to come whether the bar was open or not. She has staff who has been there since her father ran it. They're more than capable of handling it on their own. But luck should have it somebody rented it for a private event for the night. So, it's not available."

"Oh," she said. "Well that worked out."

"Yeah. So, we're going to go back to the complex and having a party there. Gus is pretty psyched about my win, and the results for the last couple of races. We've earned a lot of points this season, and sponsors are basically knocking down our doors trying to get their names associated with Freeman Racing," I said.

"That's amazing," Maya said. She hugged me tight again, and when she stepped back, I noticed her fingertips lingered in mine.

"So, you'll come with me to the party?" I asked.

"Are you sure it's okay?" she asked. "They aren't going to feel like I'm intruding?"

"No," I said, perhaps with a bit too much emphasis. "I keep telling you. They all like you very much. We would love to have you there to celebrate with us. I know the girls love adding another to their group. You'll probably even get a chance to meet Nick's girlfriend, Bryn. She wasn't at dinner last week."

"I think I saw her this week at the bar," Maya said. "At least, there was a girl there with Nick, and they looked pretty friendly. If I wasn't seeing Bryn, then I just uncovered some massive family drama I should probably keep to myself."

I laughed. "I'm sure it was Bryn. They go up to the bar together a lot. Will you come with me?"

"Yes," Maya finally said. "I will come, but I actually have my truck. I can drive, if that's okay with you."

"Sounds great. Let's go."

The party was already in full swing by the time we got to the compound. Gus had gone on ahead of us and had music blaring and lights shining on the field. What had been just a big grassy stretch in the middle of the complex when I first started working there had gradually transformed into the heart of the entire place.

It started with a couple of picnic tables, then a pavilion. From there, he added lights and a hidden sound system. The initial appearance was that it was still just a normal field with the added features of the pavilion and the picnic tables. Gus had made sure the new details didn't take away from the original appeal of the space. One of the reasons we all loved it so much was because it was so green and beautiful.

While we all loved racing and being around motorcycles, sometimes getting a break and feeling surrounded by nature rather than just being in a garage or out on a track was refreshing.

I had a feeling the trucks hadn't even been unpacked and were sitting by the garage waiting for us to get to them. Gus had gone straight into celebration mode. The trophies Darren and I won were sitting on one of the tables, and it looked like a bar's worth of beer filled multiple large inflatable coolers positioned around the edge of the field.

"How did he do this so fast?" Maya asked as we walked out into the middle of the party in progress.

"I have no idea," I said. "Sometimes things happen here that defy logic and reason. I have a feeling there is a fairly complex and potentially secretive phone tree that exists for just such purposes."

"A secret phone tree?" Maya asked. "That's pretty next-level stuff."

"You never know what you could be getting into around here," I said.

Maya shook her head and laughed. I gathered her up in my arms, spinning her around before putting her down so we could dance. It only lasted a few perfect moments before somebody shouted out that the pizza was there.

We stepped away from each other and watched as delivery drivers carried armfuls of pizza boxes onto the field and over to the picnic tables. They spread them out and Merry, Lindsey, Kelly, and Bryn walked over to start opening the boxes up. Vince came up behind Lindsey and leaned down to kiss the side of her neck. He murmured something into her ear, and she nodded. She said something to Kelly beside her, and the other woman looked over to see Remy where he was playing with Nick.

Vince and Lindsey wandered off toward the garage, and Maya and I made our way over to the tables. It looked like whoever had ordered pizza ordered one with every combination of toppings they could think of.

We all looked around and realized we didn't have any plates or napkins. I figured that's why Lindsey and Vince went down to the garage to get. There was a small storage room at the back that held extra items so if there was an event on property, we didn't have to go all the way up to the main building to get supplies.

They came back a few minutes later carrying plates, cups, and napkins. Vince was carrying the guitar that usually stayed in the breakroom. Soon, we were all lounging around eating, drinking, and listening to Vince strum on the guitar.

I kept looking over at Maya throughout the evening. She had made fast friends with the other women and was soon hanging out with them. Every now and then I got a meaningful smile or a wink from one of those women.

When that happened, I tried to stay as neutral as possible. I knew what it looked like to have Maya there at the race and with me during the celebration by the track, then here at the complex with me. I could tell what everybody was thinking, and even possibly what they were wanting.

I knew I wanted it. It was a struggle to come to terms with that realization, but I finally couldn't fight it anymore. I wanted her, but I knew she didn't want me, so I fought as hard as I could to control how I felt about her.

Nibbling on a piece of veggie pizza because he wouldn't allow himself the meat and heavier cheese, Colby, Darren's best friend, came up beside me. He must have noticed exactly how I was looking at Maya because he burst into a tirade of jokes and teasing.

It didn't much matter to me. All I was focused on was her. As long as she didn't overhear it and get upset, I would happily take the ribbing if it meant she was there with me.

17

MAYA

The party at the compound was an absolute blast. I couldn't remember ever laughing that much. And it wasn't just how much I was laughing and how much fun I was having that took me by surprise. Throughout the night, I couldn't help but notice how much Greg was watching me.

He seemed drawn into everything I was doing, but not in a strange or controlling way. More like he was just making sure I was comfortable and didn't want to take his eyes off me. I felt them on me virtually every moment of the night. And I wasn't the only one who noticed. Both Kelly and Lindsey mentioned it to me.

I figured if they knew him at all, they wouldn't lie about it. So, I pointedly didn't drink much. I enjoyed a single beer that I sipped and nursed throughout the night. There was no need for me to create any confusion.

The last thing I wanted that night was confusion. I had plans for when we got home, and none of them involved me and not knowing what was going on or not being in control of my body.

I didn't say anything to any of the women. This wasn't about them or the validation that we might get by letting everybody know something was brewing between us. Instead, I kept it quiet and just continued to enjoy the night. Finally, it was time to head home.

I hadn't noticed Greg drinking much, so I wasn't uncomfortable when it came time to climb in my dad's truck and head back to the apartment. In my original envisioning of the night we would spend together, I was dignified and in control. I moved slowly and wooed him into wanting to be with me.

Apparently, imagination me had far more self-control then actual me. As soon as the door closed behind us at the apartment, I pounced on him. I pressed against him with my chest until he was up against the door and brought my lips to within just an inch or two of his.

"Why are you staring at me?" I asked. "Huh? See something new?"

My mind nearly went blank when Greg cupped his hands around my face and leaned forward to kiss me.

"Not new," he said softly, searching my eyes.

The kiss absolutely blew my mind, but there was still enough left to be completely shocked when Greg lifted me up into his arms and carried me off to the bedroom.

I felt his arms wrap around my waist, and suddenly I was airborne. A laugh bubbled up out of my chest as he walked me backward toward his bedroom, kicking the door open and plopping me down on the bed. I bounced back up to my feet, clawing at his shirt, my lips searching for his skin and finding it on his neck. His hands roamed across my back, down my waist, and cupped my ass, pulling me to him and squeezing. I raised up on my toes as he did and finally got the buttons of his shirt open.

Greg wore a soft cotton undershirt underneath, and I ran my fingertips across it, feeling the toned body beneath. The rippling muscles that caused divots in his shirt and raised his chest felt strong and thick under my touch. Trailing kisses down his neck to his chest, I pulled on the hem of the shirt, and he helped me to remove it. Tossing it aside, it wrapped around a lampshade and dimmed the light in the room even more. I didn't mind.

"Your turn," he muttered, his voice low and husky, and a tingle went down my spine.

I stepped back, letting my eyes take in the majesty of his chiseled chest and abdomen. I pulled on the bottom of my shirt and yanked it over my head, letting it fall by my side, and our eyes made contact again. The heat in that gaze was like an inferno, and it only broke when I reached behind me to unhook my bra. As my heavy, heaving breasts tumbled out of the cups, his eyes trailed down, and a groan of appreciation rumbled out of him. I smiled and tossed the bra away, and he closed the space between us with one step.

Taking my chin in his hand, he pulled me up to kiss him again. The kiss was soft, and patient, but had a white-hot desire behind it. He wanted to take his time, to appreciate my body and this moment, and I felt the heat from my core burn through me. His kiss lasted at once for just a moment and for hours. Time was lost in the embrace, and suddenly it felt like nothing else existed but that room, that moment.

His lips moved across my cheek and down the slope of my neck. I felt his tongue brush across my collarbone and took in a breath. Kneeling in front of me, he let his tongue slide between my breasts and then sweep low under one. Inch by inch, he rose to the sensitive, taut nipple and took it into his warm mouth. A strong grip covered the other and kneaded me, and I moaned at his touch.

A free hand slid up one of my legs, and I stepped apart to give him better access. As his fingers traced my thigh, I hitched another breath and groaned loudly when they brushed my hot, wet core to run up the area between my leg and my hip to the waistband. Now with both hands, he pulled my pants down, and the cool air on my pussy caused me to break out in goose bumps. He dropped the pants and the panties together onto the floor, and I kicked out of them. I was naked, and his kisses began to trail down to the newly nude area of my body.

I let one hand slide through his silky hair as he kissed down the center of my belly until he reached the mound underneath. I gasped when his tongue slid out to sweep across my lips and then cried out when they slid through my folds, yelping in ecstasy as he found my clit. He encouraged it, teasing it with the tip of his tongue, and suddenly I felt the pressure of a thick finger sliding into my opening.

I held his head in place as his finger brushed across the top wall of my pussy and his tongue lapped me up. I was barely holding on, the tension so immediate inside of me that I felt like I was about to lose control already. Pressing down on him, pushing him into me, he took the silent guidance and his tongue moved faster, his fingers sliding in and out of me. I shook as I came, my legs vibrating and collapsing as I fell back to sit on the bed and pulled his face until he stood over me, gaining a few moments of relief from the overwhelming sensation.

His lips pressed into mine, and I slid my tongue inside his mouth to match his. I could hear him unbuttoning and unzipping his pants, and when the kiss broke, he stood up straight. I let my eyes take him in, wandering down the broad shoulders to his cut chest and ripped abs, down to the v that delineated where his hips began. As his pants dropped to the ground, my eyes widened, and I moaned as his massive, thick cock sprung out at me. He was hard and long. I reached for him, wrapping my fingers around his incredible staff and stroking him.

Grasping my ankles, he pulled me to the edge of the bed, but I sat up. Before he could fuck me, I wanted to return the favor. Placing my lips on his stomach before he could object, I kissed down his center until I reached the base of his cock. I felt his hand slide under my hair to hold the back of my head, tendrils falling between his fingers. I let my tongue slide out and trace down his shaft until it reached the head and swirled around it. He let out a grumbling sound from deep in his chest, and it encouraged me to press forward. Wondering if I could fit him into my mouth whole, I wrapped my lips around his head and let my tongue brush underneath. Then, I slid forward, taking him deep into my mouth.

His cock brushed the back of my throat, and there was still enough to grip with one hand. I dared not push him any further down and instead slid back, stroking him as I did. He did not guide my movement, but his hand balled with my hair as if to encourage me to continue. I did, taking him again into my mouth deeply, letting my free hand gently massage his balls. As my speed increased, so did his moans of pleasure, and I felt the adrenaline of my aching, hot core press me on.

Feeling like I couldn't take it anymore, I let him slide out of my mouth with an audible pop and looked up at him, our eyes swimming in each other again. He nodded back toward the top of the bed, where the pillows were, and I grinned. Shimmying back to the pillows, I let my legs fall apart and put my hands on the mattress.

He climbed onto the bed, never taking his eyes off me,

roaming across my body and making me feel like the sexiest thing he had ever seen. The feeling was mutual. This time, when he reached forward and grabbed my ankles, I let him pull me down and closer to him. He curled over top of me, his cock brushing through my folds as it searched for my opening. My breasts pressed up into his rock-hard chest, and I felt delightfully smothered by him. Letting my ankles cross behind his back, I prepared myself as he found the dripping slit and plunged deeply into me.

For a second, I couldn't exhale, and stars danced in my vision while my eyes clenched shut. An explosion of sensation, somewhere blurring the lines between discomfort and pleasure, filled me from top to bottom, and when I gained the ability to make sound, I cried out. He held himself there but for a moment to let me get used to his girth, and then he rocked back and drove even deeper into me. I simultaneously wanted to push him away and pull him deeper. But this time he waited, letting me adjust, the walls of my pussy forming around him.

Slowly he rocked into me, punctuating every thrust with an appreciative sound from deep inside his chest. My hands trailed across his back, and soon the pressure built back up and I felt like I was on the verge of an orgasm so strong it would shatter me into a million pieces. I clenched my legs around him, and my voice rose higher in pitch as his thrusts got harder, faster, and more desperate. He was closing in on a climax, too, and the knowledge that we were going to come together drove me even deeper into the spiral. Suddenly, the wave crashed over me, and I cried out as he sank into me and his body went stiff. His cock pulsed and throbbed as he came hard, and my body drained him.

18

GREG

The first thought when I woke up Sunday with Maya beside me was maybe I should have regretted it. She was the one who initiated everything, but that didn't change that we had done the one thing we were never supposed to do. Not that we ever discussed it, but there was an unspoken agreement. We were friends, and that was it.

Our friendship had to transcend everything else, even if that was searing attraction and undeniable desire. We had only ventured close to even discussing that agreement one time. Just one time in our entire friendship, and it was a disaster. It went so poorly, in fact, for the last five years I had let Maya believe I didn't even remember having the conversation with her.

And yet, here we ended up. When she rolled over and her warm, naked body pressed against mine, all that regret went away because I drowned it in desire. And I overrode all feelings of regret by kissing her.

I was so wrapped up in her that I didn't even bother to go to the garage on Sunday. It didn't upset me to think about the equipment still sitting around in the trucks, or my bike not getting cleaned and fixed immediately. For the first time ever, I didn't have the compulsion to completely dismantle the week before so that I could start a new one fresh.

Being there with Maya was so much more important.

But then I woke up Monday morning right back in the well of potential regrets. I opened my eyes while she continued to sleep beside me. Maybe I manipulated her and took advantage of her still-fragile state. After all, she was scared and alone, and I offered her not only a place to live and be taken care of, but also friends and a pseudo family.

It would be easy to see where something like that could be seen as manipulation. Maybe she tumbled into bed with me because of built-up emotion, pain, and anger, and a desire to get back at Marshall. Wasn't it the old adage that the fastest way to get over somebody was to get under somebody else?

Was that what was going on here?

At the same time, waking up with Maya cuddled up in my arms and her head rested on my chest after an entire day and night of lovemaking was pretty much the best outcome I could ever think of, so I couldn't bring myself to really regret it. This was a moment I had been thinking about for years, even if I never said it. Even if I never even allowed myself to fully come to terms with it and admit it to myself, it was something I'd wanted for a long time.

I had to wait for Maya to wake up so I could see how she felt about it. This could really go either way. It was possible as soon as she was conscious and didn't have the option of just lying in bed with me for the rest of the day, reality would strike. She could think through what happened between us over the course of the last thirty-six hours and decide she had made a mistake.

Or, she could be as happy about it as I was. The only

real way to know was to ask her. She was still sleeping soundly in my arms, and I didn't want to move. I didn't want to disturb her, and I especially didn't want to hasten her waking up and having that conversation if it was going to end badly. I just wanted to savor these moments for as long as they lasted.

It didn't take much longer. She stretched, sliding languidly against the sheets and nuzzling her face down deeper into my chest. As she woke up, she tilted her head to look into my face. She blinked up at me, and a grin slid up across her lips.

"Good morning," she murmured.

"Good morning," I said softly. "You don't need to get up yet. Get some more sleep. I have to get up and go to work, but you should rest."

And it was all she needed to hear. Her eyes fluttered shut again, and it seemed that before I even got to my feet, she was deeply asleep again. She needed that rest. It was Monday, and she was due at the bar that night. If she didn't get enough sleep, she wouldn't be able to stick around all night and do what needed to be done.

I leaned down and touched a kiss to the middle of her forehead, then one to her lips before heading to the compound. I wasn't particularly looking forward to getting to the garage. Unloading the truck and putting away all the equipment wasn't my most favorite activity. It felt almost like a tease. I spent hours unloading everything but wasn't able to actually ride.

One thing I had going for me was that my second bike was coming along extremely well. It wouldn't be too much longer before it was finished, and I would be able to take it out onto the back roads to enjoy it. While I was designing it for the purpose of having a secondary race bike that could be used for specific tracks or riding techniques, I also wanted to be able to really have fun with it.

Unpacking the equipment was the perfect opportunity to talk to Gus and Kelly about the bike and get their input. I didn't want them doing it for me or taking it over like a project. But I also didn't want to take up time they needed for their own work. That meant walking back and forth hauling supplies and equipment was a chance to talk about it without it being a distraction.

I knew neither one of them would see it that way. If I asked for more help and input than they were already giving me, they would happily offer it. And if they were going too far and I told them to back down a little so I could do it myself, they would without question. I just never wanted to upset any of them.

Almost as soon as I got to the garage, Merry cornered me. The look in her eyes told me she wasn't just coming to have a friendly chat.

"Is Maya okay?" she asked.

"What do you mean, is she okay? Why wouldn't she be?" I asked.

"Just wanted to know," she said. "With everything that's been going on, I know she's been going through a lot."

"That's true," I said.

This was a weird conversation, and I wasn't sure where she was going with it.

"So, I noticed the two of you missing from the family barbeque. Were you giving her a skewer of your own at home?" she asked.

And there it was. It was actually pretty impressive. As soon as she got that question out, a smirk came across her face.

I shook my head at her. "Are you trying to mess with my love life, Merry?"

She shrugged and gave a dramatic toss of her hair. "Maybe. It wouldn't be the worst thing in the world, you know."

"What wouldn't?" I asked.

I knew what she was getting at, but I wanted to hear it straight from her. She needed to clarify it and lay everything right out. Mostly because I liked seeing her get squirmy when she wasn't expecting something like that.

"Being with Maya," she said. "Being with anybody. It would be nice to just see you in a relationship. If it so happened to be with the gorgeous women that you keep insisting to everybody is just your best friend, then who's to argue?"

I shook my head and refused to further feed into it. I got to the garage and poured myself into work. If I put all my focus and attention on unloading the equipment and doing the post-race cleaning and fixing to my bike, I wouldn't think about Maya.

And that was exactly what I needed to be doing right then. I needed to not think about Maya or what it could mean. That day and a half together was absolutely incredible, but there were still so many lingering doubts and questions. I didn't want to dig into what happened between us or how I felt about her.

It was too much. Letting myself think about it right now felt like it could make everything explode, and I desperately didn't want that to happen. I prepared myself to field more questions. The vast majority of the time, if one of my extended honorary family was talking about something, it meant the rest of them knew about it.

Merry was asking about Maya because at the very least,

all the women wanted to know. It looked like they had gotten close quickly, and they wanted to know everything they could about her, and our relationship.

But she could have also been sent by any of the Freeman boys. They didn't like to admit how curious they were about things, but they definitely were. They didn't consider it gossip if they heard it from their wives or girl-friends. It was a neat little mental trick they managed to make work for them.

For the rest of the day, I poured myself fully into my work, so I didn't think about how much I wanted to go home and get Maya back in my bed.

19

MAYA

Opening my eyes again Monday morning, I vaguely remembered waking up earlier. I remembered looking over and seeing Greg getting out of bed so he could get ready for work. I smiled at him, but I didn't think I said anything. Not that there were really any words to say at that point.

The only ones he could think of were to tell me to go back to sleep because I didn't have to get up for work yet. It didn't bother me. It was actually sweet of him to want to make sure I was getting enough rest, but when I woke up for the second time and realized it was late in the morning, the whole situation felt weird.

Shouldn't he have said something else? Or shouldn't I have said something else?

Should he have kissed me goodbye? Should I have walked him to the door?

There were so many questions bouncing around in my head, and I didn't know how to answer any of them. This was completely uncharted territory. I mean, it was Greg and that wasn't the kind of relationship we had ever ventured into.

I didn't know how to navigate what was feeling like essentially an extended one-night stand. Especially when it happened with my best friend and in our own home. All those overlapping sets of rules and etiquette made for some serious confusion.

I went into the kitchen and peeked into the refrigerator. There was no packed lunch for me, but he had put a plate of leftovers from the day before when we ordered Indian food at the front of a shelf with a blank sticky note on it. That wasn't exactly what I was hoping for. I needed some kind of sign, something to tell me how he was feeling and what he was thinking.

I had no texts from him, no missed calls. I didn't know if he regretted what happened between us or not. I made him dinner anyway and tucked it into the refrigerator with his usual pink sticky note. I hesitated for a few seconds before I drew the heart on it. I didn't know if he would see that heart differently now. Or if it meant something different at all.

Eventually, I drew it anyway. This was our tradition. It was what I did, and I didn't want to do anything different and have him think it might mean something. More than anything, I hoped I hadn't messed up our friendship completely.

I got ready for work and headed into the bar a little bit early, not wanting to be at the apartment by myself. As soon as I went inside, I saw Lindsey giving me a look. That was the last thing I needed right then. I felt heat and color rush up to my cheeks, and I turned away hoping she didn't notice.

For the rest of the shift, I did my best to dodge her and all the questions and leading comments she had piled up and prepared. She seemed to love to gossip. I picked that up about her during the last couple of times we hung out, but especially during and after the race. It was never malicious. She didn't want to say bad things about people or be nasty.

Instead, she just wanted to chat and giggle, but I didn't need her chatting or giggling about Greg and me right then. She kept looking at me, searching my face like I was going to suddenly crack and spill everything. I kept quiet. I didn't feel like I needed to confirm whatever it was Lindsey thought she knew.

Especially considering that I still didn't even know what Greg was thinking. I didn't want to talk about anything until he and I had smoothed things out.

I didn't bring the Indian food with me to the bar. So later when I was on my break, I asked the cook to make me a burger. Sitting at the corner of the bar, chomping down on the delicious food, I got a text. Pulling my phone out of my pocket, I saw it was from Greg. It was just a picture of his empty plate and "thank you," but it was a relief. It felt like a good thing that he was reaching out at all.

And this was when I decided we could still be friends if that was all he wanted. What happened between us could be put behind us, and we would just carry on the way we always had. He was still so precious to me, and even if there could be nothing else between us, I didn't want to lose him completely.

I tried to put it all out of my mind so I could focus on work, but it stayed with me all night. I kept finding myself looking up for the door, waiting for him to come in. He never did, and I did my best to stop thinking about it. Finally, the night ended, and I was able to get out from under the inquisitive eyes of Lindsey and head home.

Just like he always was, Greg was asleep when I got

back to the apartment. I briefly considered going into his room and sliding into bed with him. I wanted to be close to him and feel his arms around me again. But I stopped myself. I wouldn't do that without his invitation. While it might seem like a fun surprise if I knew he wanted me there, if he didn't, it could end badly.

If I had any hope of us being able to maintain the friendship we had, I had to steady myself and let him give me the cues. We were in a strange position. I showed up without any notice and threw myself on his mercy. I completely depended on the hope that even with the distance and strain in our relationship over the last five years, that he would still have the loyalty and heart for me that he always did.

Greg had scooped me up, swept up the broken pieces, and brought me into his home. Without question or hesitation, he gave me a chance at a new life. And now we were in this odd place. We had crossed a line that had never been crossed before, and we had to figure out where that put us.

It was possible that once reality kicked in it was time for me to get up on my own two feet. If that was the case, I would accept it and wouldn't want to make him feel strange about it. After all, he had no obligation to me. We didn't make any agreements, and the landlord still hadn't gotten around to giving him a new lease.

I felt like if I kept pushing, it would make Greg more uncomfortable. If he wasn't feeling anything toward me, or worse, feeling regret about what happened between us, me continuing to try to maintain that connection would only create awkwardness. I knew Greg well enough to know he wouldn't want to hurt me worse than I already was. After what Marshall just put me through, he wouldn't want to suddenly tell me I needed to leave.

I went into my room and dropped down onto my bed. Lying there reminded me that I needed to add up my tips and make sure I had the money for the next payment for my bedroom set. Eventually, I would pay Greg back for putting the down payments down for me and helping me cover the other expenses of getting my room set up.

He said he wanted to do it, and he kept insisting it was important to him that I felt at home and comfortable there, but it was still my bed and should be my responsibility. It would take me some time to catch all the way back up and be able to get to a point where I could make those payments, help him with rent, buy my own food, and do all those things I was already so used to doing.

It made me feel bad to even think about, but the disparity in my income between working at the Cabinet Factory and at the bar was becoming more obvious. I would have to be extremely careful about budgeting and sticking to that budget if I wanted to stay ahead.

There might come a time when Greg and I no longer lived together, and I wanted to be ready to strike out on my own. It reminded me I still needed to go to the bank and get my account set up. It was something I still hadn't done. It kept slipping my mind, but my sock full of tips was getting thicker, and soon I would get my first paycheck. I wanted to make sure I had an account to keep it in.

20

GREG

I lay awake, waiting for Maya to get home from the bar. It was hours after I was usually awake, but I couldn't force myself to go to sleep. I needed to know she was home safe. I also wanted to see how she was going to react to me when she did.

I positioned myself on the side of the bed, leaving space open beside me and a pillow empty for her. On Sunday we just naturally tumbled into bed together, and I wondered if that was going to be the way it was going to be between us now. If she would just ease into that position in my life so we would never have to really talk it through.

Maybe that didn't sound realistic. Maybe I should have just expected that we would have to actually confront what happened and figure it out. Yet, I could still hope. And when I heard her come in late that night, I waited. She walked down the hallway, and for a few seconds, her footsteps paused. She was standing still outside my door, and I wondered if she was considering whether to come in.

Part of me wanted to call out to her. I wanted to invite

her to come in and climb in bed with me, but at the same time, that might just make things more uncomfortable. I didn't know what was going through her mind. She'd left me dinner just like she always did, but I didn't get a response from the text message I sent her after eating when I came home from work.

Again, I found myself wanting to go to the bar but couldn't bring myself to do it. So instead, I lay awake and just waited for her to get home, hoping things would unfold on their own. But they didn't. She started walking again, and I heard the door to her bedroom close. It took me a while longer to fall asleep, but I finally did.

I woke up groggy and definitely feeling the effects of the missing hours of sleep while I'd waited for Maya to come home. I stood in the shower for longer than I usually did, hoping the water would cut through the fog and wake me up. I was in a rush to get out of the apartment and to the compound, but I took the time to make her lunch. I felt bad for just leaving the leftovers the day before and didn't want to do that again.

Just before leaving, I carefully opened the door to her room so it didn't make too much noise and peered inside. She was stretched out across her bed, sleeping deeply. I watched her for a few seconds, and right then I knew I couldn't just wait for the world to happen for me. This wasn't just going to unravel itself. This was something she and I had to talk about.

The last time we let something go unspoken, it ended up with us losing touch for five years. And that was what brought us here to this moment, but I wasn't willing to risk another five years without her. Or even worse, that if she walked away, I would never see her again. I needed to be up-front and honest with her, no matter how it was going to fall into place.

I went back into the kitchen and grabbed my sticky notes. I wrote her a note telling her I would stop by Lindsey's bar for dinner, so she didn't need to make me anything. I thought about that for a second, then added that I wouldn't object to some dessert, or something I could heat up for breakfast in the morning. I didn't want her to feel like I didn't appreciate what she did for me every day.

After I writing her note with great care, I went outside and headed for my bike rather than my truck.

It was definitely a day when I needed to be on the back of a motorcycle. I needed the feeling of freedom and openness. It woke up my brain and helped me think. At least I had taken a step. I was unsure where we stood or how any of this was going to work out, but I knew we needed to talk face-to-face.

Going to see her at work was definitely a risk. It was going to be busy, which meant there would be plenty of other people around. We weren't going to be alone, so it wasn't a setting for the most personal and private details of the conversation we needed to have. It would definitely break the ice. Going in to see her would let us get close to each other and start talking on a neutral level.

From there, we could figure out what to do next.

I was grateful to not have anybody swoop down on me when I got to the racing complex. I got a few questioning looks from Kelly and Gus, but neither one of them said anything. That was a relief. I wasn't going to get into any of this with them before I had a chance to talk to Maya. They seemed to understand that, and we didn't talk about anything but work for the entire day.

I expected the day to drag by slowly as time tended to

do when there was something at the end you were looking ahead to.

But surprisingly work moved way faster than I thought it would, and soon I was pulling into the bar parking lot. For the most part, I didn't usually drink often. And when I did, it was almost never more than one or two beers at a time. Having an alcoholic father had a lasting effect on me, and as a result his addiction destroyed my life. It made me very aware of the effects of alcohol and also my inborn proclivity toward abusing it.

It felt strange to walk in without everybody else around me. Lindsey looked up from behind the bar and waved, then pointed to a free stool. I sat down, and she smiled at me.

"Hey, there," she said. "What brings you by here tonight?"

It was definitely a leading question. She wanted as much information as I could give her. But unfortunately for her, that was nothing.

"I just thought I would stop by," I said. "Maybe grab something to eat."

"Sure thing," she said. "I'll get you a menu."

She went into the kitchen, and a few seconds later, the door opened and Maya came out. She was in her uniform of jeans and a tight black V-neck T-shirt. It was simple but devastating. I couldn't take my eyes off her, and I didn't even try.

She handed me the menu; her eyes locked on mine.

"Hey," I said.

"Hey."

"Can you take a break?" I asked.

She glanced back toward the kitchen, then nodded. "Sure."

We went over to one of the booths in the back of the bar, and Lindsey came by. She took our orders and walked away slower than I had seen another human walk in a long time.

"She is trying desperately to figure out what is going on between us," I said, trying to laugh and sound casual.

Maya nodded. "So am I."

One of the barbacks came up at that moment and handed each of us a drink. A beer for me and a glass of iced tea with lemon for Maya since she was still technically on the clock. She took that moment as a break in the conversation to detour on to another topic.

"How was your day?" she asked.

"It was good," I said, realizing now wasn't the time to get into anything personal. For right now, we needed to just be in the same space. We needed to be able to talk about anything and everything else before we could hope to talk about us.

We fell into a conversation that started tense but then became more comfortable and natural. As we ate, things felt normal again. I lingered as long as I felt like I could before getting up.

"I should probably go and stop distracting you," I said. "I'm sure Lindsey would like to have her employee back."

"Probably," Maya said. "Thanks for coming by. This was fun."

"Absolutely," I said. "Maybe we'll pick a day once a week for me to do that."

"I'd like that," she said.

I started to leave, then turned around. "Come into my room when you get home?"

A bright shock of color went across her cheeks, and she glanced away, then nodded. She came over and gave me a quick kiss before rushing away toward the kitchen. As I walked toward the door, I glanced back at the bar and saw Lindsey. She had a huge grin across her face and gave me a salute. I laughed and went out to my bike. I headed home feeling a bit better about everything.

21

MAYA

I got home dead tired and feeling like I could barely put one foot in front of the other. This job was a blessing, and I was actually really enjoying it, but it was exhausting. Especially when I was doing everything I could to not just stand around and think about Greg. And that meant hopping from task to task as fast as I could. At the end of the night, it left me dragging.

But at least I had the best place possible to drag myself to. I got to the apartment and didn't hesitate to walk straight to Greg's bedroom. I thought he might be awake waiting for me, but he was sleeping peacefully, and that actually seemed better. It was nice coming home to something so comforting.

Standing in the blue moonlight coming through his window, I stripped down to nothing but my underwear before sliding in next to him. He had left the side of the bed I took over during the weekend open, which warmed my heart and made me feel for sure he wanted me there and hadn't just said it.

It might have been weird. It probably would have

sounded weird to anybody who heard it. And it probably should have been weird. And yet, it wasn't. Slipping between the cool sheets and nuzzling up against Greg felt so natural it was as if I'd been doing it every night of my life.

I let out a sigh as he moved to wrap his arm around me and held me close. Not letting anything else come into my mind, I closed my eyes and let sleep pull me in.

Him getting out of bed at some point later woke me up even though he was trying to be slow and gentle so he didn't jostle me. I opened my eyes to look at him, and he smiled.

"Go on back to sleep," he said. "You don't need to be up yet."

It was the same thing he'd said to me Monday morning, but it felt completely different now. He walked into the bathroom, and I heard the shower turn on. Glancing at my phone, I checked the time. Five hours of sleep was good enough. I slipped out of bed and took off my panties, letting them fall to the floor with the rest of my clothes.

Moving quietly so he wouldn't hear me, I snuck into the bathroom and slipped stealthily into the shower behind him.

If he didn't know I was behind him, he was good at acting like he wasn't surprised. Rather than jumping or acting shocked, he turned with a grin on his face and water running down into the curve of his lips. I stepped into him, and he pulled me in, the water spreading across my back and down my legs, and my breasts pressed against his chest. They rubbed against his hardened, wet muscles, and my nipples went taut.

One hand slid down to cup my ass, and I grinned into a kiss that had me melt into his body. I could feel his thick cock harden as it pressed against my stomach, and I let one hand slide down his body while our tongues tangled to wrap around the base of him. The hot water made him slick in my grip, and I stroked him up toward his belly for a moment, looking down to marvel at it before kissing him again.

His skin smelled fresh and clean as I kissed down his chest, making my way to my knees. He pushed his back against the shower wall and let one hand slide through my now soaking hair. When I reached his cock, I let my tongue trail around the base, taking a moment to fill my mouth with his balls while I stroked him. He let out a groan as I switched from one to the other, and I slid my tongue up the center and all the way to the head of his cock.

I wrapped my lips around him and breathed out through my nose before taking him deeply onto my tongue. When the tip reached the back of my throat, I choked and pulled back. The sound of my struggles to take him deeply into my mouth seemed to make him harder, and I repeated the action, noticing the grip on my hair tighten as I went as far down as I could go. Suddenly, he pulled back on my hair, and I followed the guidance. Curling my lips so they pulled easily on his cock, I let my hands drop and submitted to his desire.

His hips rocked back and forth into me as he fucked my mouth, and I relaxed my throat after a few moments. No longer was I gagging, but taking him farther and farther in, until my lips pressed on the skin of his core. Pulling me back and off him, he leaned down and pressed his lips into mine for a passionate kiss.

"Your turn," he grumbled, and I giggled as I stood quickly.

But rather than kneel in front of me, he put his hands on my shoulders and turned me away, pushing me into the wall of the shower. He knelt behind me, pulled my hips toward him, and squatted down, sliding his legs between mine so I stood above him. He wasted no time as his tongue slid through my folds from underneath, and I moaned in pleasure. I pressed my hands into the walls as he let his mouth play over my core, his tongue teasing at my clit before sliding through and into my opening. His hands grasped at my ass and squeezed, pulling at it so he could gain greater access.

Seeing an opportunity, I bent even further and let one hand slide down. I filled my fingers with his cock as he licked me, and I felt the vibration of his groan on my pussy. I squealed at the sensation, and he responded by doing it again. This time his tongue pressing against my clit. I could feel the tension rising and knew the overwhelming sensory overload of the hot water splashing down on my back, his tongue playing with my clit and my hand wrapped around his cock, was enough to make me reach a climax. I bore down into it, and suddenly the tension exploded. I came, my legs shaking as he lapped me up, pulling me into his face with both hands.

In the height of the orgasm, he suddenly stood, and I had only a moment to prepare myself before he slammed into me. The feeling of his huge cock filling me was intense and immediate, and I shouted out into the pouring water. My face turned up, and the shower rained down on me as he reared back and slammed into me again. Strong fingers curled around the curve of my hips and pulled me into him again, and soon he was fucking me in a steady rhythm. I tried to press into the wall of the shower for control, but there was none to be had. Greg had me right where he wanted me, and I was helpless to change it.

As if I wanted to.

Soon the rhythm evened, and I was able to breathe

normally again, the lights dancing in my eyelids fading away when I shut them. I pushed my hips back into him with every thrust, and he growled with the intensity of the movement. The sound sent a thrill down my spine, and I looked over my shoulder at him. Biting my bottom lip to keep from crying out again, I watched as his eyes trailed to my backside, where he watched his cock disappear into me. Then he looked up, and our eyes met, and a grin crossed his lips.

He pulled himself out of me and turned me around. I went willingly, prepared to go anywhere, be in any position he asked. I was his for the taking. He pressed my back against the wall, lifting one of my legs under his arm so I stretched my hips open for him. This allowed him to put his other arm around me and press his body close as the shower poured down on both of us. He positioned himself at my opening and slid inside easily, my pussy ready and waiting for him.

The movements were slower now, more methodical, but no less passionate. We kissed under the water, his cock sliding in and out of me, filling me and giving my body the attention it so desperately wanted. As I was on the brink of another climax, he pulled out of me and took my hand, leading me out of the shower.

We stepped into the surprisingly warm bathroom. He led me to the long counter along the wall and turned to me. Picking me up and placing my ass on the counter, he stepped between my legs. Folding his arms under my legs, he pulled me to the edge of the counter and slid inside me again.

I wrapped my hands around his neck, holding myself in place and letting my head rest for a moment on the wide mirror behind me. He turned a little, and I looked back into the reflection and felt myself getting somehow even more turned on watching him fuck me. My hair was wet and in thick strings on my face, and water dripped from both of our bodies, but something about this position in this place sent me into overdrive.

He thrust into me with an animalistic fury, and I knew he was getting close. Once or twice, I saw him glance at the mirror, too, and I lay back across the counter so my breasts would jiggle with each thrust. He reached forward with one hand and cupped one, as if he was using it for leverage to plunge into me, and I felt the wave about to crest of another intense orgasm.

My voice rose with each thrust, and my ankles tightening around his waist as he fucked me harder and more intensely. I could see the passion in his eyes, the reverence of my naked body, the longing for release, and I willed myself to hold on for just a moment longer. I wanted us to experience that ecstasy together. But the wave was crashing over me, and I was powerless to stop it. My voice rose to outright screaming yelps, and suddenly my world exploded in an earth-shattering climax, my toes curling as his cock slammed harder, deeper into me. In the midst of the wave, another higher one washed over me as he growled and exploded inside me. We came together, pulsing with each other, our bodies giving and taking.

I struggled for breath as he continued to pound into me until he was empty, and then he collapsed into my chest on the counter. I kissed his forehead and traced my fingers along his back as our breathing returned to normal and I gained control over my legs again.

A few minutes later after stepping back into the shower and washing off, we managed to get out of the bathroom, and I wrapped up in a towel while Greg got dressed for work. I walked him to the front door and kissed him goodbye. As soon as I closed the door behind him, I went right back into the bedroom and curled back up in the spot still warm from his body. Five hours might be enough, but seven or eight was definitely better. Especially when I was so relaxed. Closing my eyes, I smiled into the pillow and started to drift away, happier than I'd ever been.

GREG

The sky was threatening rain when I walked out of the apartment into the parking lot, so I opted to take my truck to work rather than hopping on the back of my motorcycle. If the weather had allowed it, today definitely would have been a morning to enjoy a ride. As therapeutic as riding when I was upset or angry could be, it was even better when my mood was as high as it was that day. It felt like I was soaring, and I just wanted to keep the rush going.

Even without the bike ride, I still ended up getting to the garage with a grin on my face so big it stretched my cheeks. I sat in the parking lot for a few seconds trying to bring it down a notch, but there was no use. This high wasn't going away anytime soon. Not after a morning like that coming after a night spent with Maya in my arms.

Her coming home and climbing into bed with me woke me up, but it was more than worth it. I would happily miss out on some of my REM cycles to have her there in my bed with me every night. And it was exactly what I intended. That second bedroom could go right back to being just a spare room now. Maybe a guest room. Or a room that was just for fun if we wanted a new setting.

My steps were almost bouncing when I made my way down to the garage. Darren was crouched down on the floor tinkering with his bike when I walked in. He looked over at me and smiled, shaking his head.

"I was all geared up to make fun of you for not being here earlier than the rest of us, but that stupid grin on your face tells me you really wouldn't care," he said.

"No, no I don't," I said. "I'll be right back. I'm going to put my jacket in my locker."

I walked around to the bank of lockers in a small room off to the side of the garage. Taking off the light jacket I'd thrown on in case the rain came, I stuffed it into the locker.

As I was standing there unloading my wallet and the bag of snacks I'd brought with me, I realized that in the distraction of the morning, I hadn't taken the time to make Maya lunch like I always did and that made me feel bad. I didn't want her to think I had just forgotten about her, or that I wasn't going to try anymore now that we seemed to be settling into a relationship.

I couldn't exactly go back to the apartment and make something for her or add her usual sticky note, but I could make sure she knew I was thinking about her. I grabbed my phone and called my favorite little pizza shop. I ordered her a pizza and a salad to be delivered, then asked the manager to make sure the delivery driver sent me a text when he arrived at the apartment.

I wanted to be able to send a message to Maya when she was getting the food as a stand-in for the note. Just doing that had me grinning all over again, and when Darren looked up at me as I walked back into the garage, he laughed and rolled his eyes.

"Still with the smile," he said. "You must have had a really good morning."

"And why would he have a good morning?" Kelly asked from the other side of the garage, widening her eyes theatrically in mock innocence.

"I don't know," Darren said. "It looks like he has a nice, healthy glow about him. Maybe he got up and took a long jog."

"Or maybe he just had some really good, hot... breakfast," Kelly teased.

Darren laughed, and I shook my head. I had a feeling I was going to get teased all to hell all day, but I didn't care. It was more than worth it. I was happy to accept the ribbing if it meant having Maya in my bed the way I never thought I would have her.

"You know what?" Darren said. "That's got to be it. And because it's just the type of guy he is, I bet he gave some to Maya, too."

"Actually, I didn't have breakfast at all," I said. "So I'm going to go up to the main building and see what Minnie has in the kitchen. I definitely have a big appetite this morning."

I walked out of the garage with both of them laughing behind me and headed out to the main building. I greeted the receptionist, and we had a short conversation before I went down the hall into the kitchen. The room almost looked like a tiny restaurant with several tables set up in the front section of the room, a large island counter set in the middle, and a full kitchen behind it.

The tables were rarely used. Most of us would rather just gather around the island and talk while we were eating. And if there wasn't anybody else in the room when we walked in, like now, then we just grabbed whatever food was available and brought it back to where we were working.

Like most mornings, the island and one of the counters was full of plates, platters, and stands full of the various treats and snacks Minette Freeman made. Minnie was known for her legendary bouts of baking. It used to be that she only really did it when she was feeling stressed or had a lot on her mind.

As her sons started getting married and having babies, though, it became a more frequent thing until she was constantly filling the kitchen with her goodies. She still went into more rapid production when there was a lot going on or she was upset about something. But since things seem to be calmer right now, there was an almost manageable amount of food.

I looked around at the offerings, trying to decide what I wanted to have for breakfast. Just looking at the baked goods made me think of Maya. Her baking skills definitely hadn't climbed up to the point of competing with the Freeman matriarch, but she was getting better. And her regular cooking never disappointed.

When I was visiting her at the bar the night before, she mentioned she wanted to send more food to the complex with me to share with everybody. I walked around the kitchen, scouting what Minnie had already made so I could give my recommendations of what she might want to make.

Carrying a plate with servings of several of the different offerings piled onto it in one hand and a cup of orange juice in the other, I headed back to the garage. Darren and Kelly were still giggling when I went back in. I sat my breakfast on the counter at the back of the garage and leaned against it to spend a couple of minutes eating.

"So, what did Lindsey tell you?" I asked.

They exchanged glances.

"I don't know what you're talking about," Darren said. "Lindsey didn't tell me anything."

"Maybe not you, but I know she talked to Kelly. Or at least she talked to Vince, who would have talked to you. Or Nick for that matter. It's like one giant game of telephone around here," I said.

They looked at each other again and burst into laughter.

I shook my head and ate a bit more, washed it down with juice, and headed over to the coffee maker. The change in my morning routine was definitely throwing off the start to my day, but I could live with that.

After a cup of coffee, I filled it again and brought it over to sit next down at my workstation. I felt happier than I had in as long as I could remember, like even if I could manage to wipe the smile off my face, it was just going to come back a few seconds later.

But my good mood didn't last.

I had been working for a couple of hours when I heard somebody clear their throat a few steps behind me. I looked over my shoulder and saw Gus looking down at me. Usually, when he came into the garage, he was cheerful, but this time, his face was drawn.

"I need to speak to you for a minute, Greg," he said.

His tone was heavy and serious. I nodded and got up. We walked outside, and I immediately saw my mother standing right outside. Her eyes were rimmed with red, and I could see streaks of tears down her cheeks. I hadn't seen her since she left Charlotte to go back to Shelby after I recovered enough to not need twenty-four-hour care.

I walked closer to her, and she fell into my arms.

"Mom, what's going on?" I asked.

"It's your father," she said, her voice wobbly and faint. "He's dead."

It didn't make sense. My father had skipped town a long time ago. As soon as he started drinking, he started spending long stretches away from the house. When he was there, it was miserable. Eventually, he left altogether. We had done just fine without him, so I didn't understand my mother's reaction.

"How did you find out?" I asked.

As far as I knew, neither of us had any contact with my father or any member of his family since the day he left for good.

"Your grandmother found me. She wanted to tell me. I'm not sure why, considering they all hated me."

Thinking about my father made my stomach turn and my heart pound a little harder in my chest. By the time I was a teenager, there would be months at a time when I didn't see him. He would leave us with nothing and come back only to brutalize my mother. Him changing the way he had and leaving me with so much instability in my life had really messed me up.

Now to find out he was dead, I didn't know how to feel. He was a human being and was once a good man, so there was some sadness, but there was also a sense of relief. I hated the confusion.

"She didn't tell you anything else?" I asked.

"Well," Mom said, stepping back from me, "I guess I do know why she contacted me. It seems your father left you something in his will."

"He left something for me?" I asked. "I didn't know he had anything to leave."

"Neither did I. I have some papers for you in my car, and there will be a will reading in a couple days," she said.

I was in shock as I followed her to the car and took the papers from her. It wasn't just trying to wrap my head around the fact that my father was dead. I was having a hard time accepting that my mother was actually this sad about it.

2 3

MAYA

I was just about to get ready for work when the door to the apartment opened. Surprised, I looked out of the kitchen and saw Greg come into the living room.

"Hey," I said happily. "What a wonderful surprise. And I thought that having a pizza delivered to me was going to be the only surprise I got today."

I started across the room to him, ready to gather him up in my arms and kiss him. It only took a few steps for me to notice the look on his face. He looked ashen and drawn, and his hair was on end like he'd been running his fingers through it. He walked straight past me and to the cabinets in the living room where he kept liquor for parties.

Opening it firmly, he reached inside and pulled out a bottle of vodka, an alarming action that made a spike of worry go up the back of my neck. Greg was far from a big drinker. Definitely not the type to come home in the middle of the day and start knocking back vodka. Something was very wrong.

He'd left for work that morning in such an incredible mood but came back hours before he was even supposed to get off looking devastated. Could he have been fired? This seemed extremely unlikely. I had been around the entire team, and they absolutely adored Greg. He worked extremely hard and put everything into not only the races, but everything else did at the complex.

It would take something huge for there to be such a sudden change that they would remove him from the team.

It had to be something else, something I couldn't even fathom. I wanted to give Greg his space, to let him work through whatever he was feeling and thinking without suffocating him. But after he had taken three long pulls from the bottle without even bothering to pour the liquor into a glass, I realized this was a more serious situation than I originally thought.

Crossing the room quickly, I put one hand on his back and pulled the bottle out of his grip with the other. I put the top back on and put the vodka away.

"What is going on?" I asked. "You never show up early, and you look like you're about to crack. Tell me what happened."

He looked into my eyes as if it was the first time he was seeing me since walking into the apartment. He let his shoulders drop and shook his head slightly. Taking his hand, I led him over to the couch and brought him to sit down with me. I didn't let go of his hand, wanting to offer him the comfort and support of me being there.

"My mother showed up at the compound today," he said.

"Oh," I said. "I didn't realize she was in town."

"She was," Greg said. "She came because my grandmother got in touch with her."

"Your grandmother?" I had never heard him talk about a grandmother. "Which grandmother?"

"My father's mother," he said. "My mother said she called to tell her that my father died."

The news struck me so hard I felt like I couldn't come up with any words for a few seconds. Everything I'd ever known about Greg's father was that he was a course, distant, and sometimes violent man. I remembered him telling me that when he was much younger, his father was very different. But that would change because of alcohol. He was around very little, didn't provide for his family, and had taken everything he could.

"He died?" I asked. "When? What happened?"

Greg shook his head. "I didn't get all the details. Apparently, it was fairly recent. Within the last week, I think. Mom said she thinks he must have had a heart attack. Heart disease ran in his family, and he didn't exactly have the healthiest lifestyle."

"Greg, I'm so sorry. I don't even know what to say."

"Neither do I," he said. "I don't even know what to *think*. Or feel. This is my dad. For everything that he did when I was a teenager, I can still remember who he was when I was little. I try not to remember it or think about it because it hurts too much. But I do. And I remember how hard it was to have him not around. And I never got a chance to talk to him again. Now he's gone."

I wrapped my arms around him and kissed his cheek. "I wish there was something I could do."

"I know," he said. "But just being here for me means everything."

"Give me just a minute. I'll be right back."

I went into the bedroom to get my phone and called Lindsey.

"Hey, what's up?"

"I don't think I'm going to be able to come in today. Can

I call a family emergency? Greg is in a really bad way," I said.

"Absolutely, that's fine," she said without hesitation. "Family is always first. You let me know if you need anything, okay?"

"I will, thank you so much."

I went back into the living room to check on Greg, then went to the kitchen. I got out a bag of potatoes I had just bought and rummaged around in drawers until I found the peeler. Bringing two large bowls with me, I went back into the living room and sat down with him. He was holding papers in his hands.

"I thought of something you could do for me," he said.

"Anything. What do you need?"

I started peeling the potatoes into one of the bowls, waiting for him to let me know what I could do to help him.

"Come with me to the lawyer's office."

"Lawyer's office?" I asked. "What do you mean?"

"Apparently, my father left me something in his will. That's why my grandmother found my mother. We have to go to the reading to get the formal information about what I inherited. But according to these papers, he left me some money."

"Wow," I said. "That's nice."

"I guess."

"You guess?"

He looked at me with a storm of emotions in his eyes. "I hadn't even spoken to this man in at least eight years. The last time I did, I was trying to beat him to a pulp. Before that, we barely exchanged words more than once or twice a year. The last I knew of him, he was an absolute bum who stole everything from my mother and left us with nothing. How could he possibly have left me money?"

"I don't know," I said. "But I will absolutely go with you. We'll find out together."

He continued to stare at the papers in his hands while I finished peeling the potatoes. When I was done, I grabbed the remote and turned on one of his favorite shows. It was just an old rerun, but I felt like he needed something mindless right then. I brought the potatoes into the kitchen and chopped them into chunks, then filled the pot with water and waited for it to boil before putting the potatoes in.

While they cooked, I sat with Greg on the couch. We didn't say anything, but I held his hand and occasionally stroked the back with my thumb. I just wanted him to know I was there, and he could depend on me. I didn't need him to talk. He didn't have to open up any more than he was ready to. I knew this had to be extremely difficult for him, and he was struggling to figure it out himself.

All I could do for him right then was let him know he wasn't alone.

When the potatoes were done cooking, I mashed them with plenty of butter and milk, added a liberal amount of salt and pepper, and topped them with warmed-up corn. It was a favorite simple meal of ours from when we were younger, something I hadn't eaten in a long time, but something told me it would bring him comfort.

Filling two massive bowls, I brought them into the living room and sat down to eat.

"He was here in Charlotte the whole time," Greg finally said an hour later.

"He was?" I asked, shocked. "And you didn't know?"

"No," Greg said. "I had no idea. I had always wanted to move here, and I didn't really know why. Maybe he mentioned it when I was younger and I don't remember, but the name of the town stuck with me. I just can't believe I have been living in the same place as him for years and we never saw each other."

He looked broken, so overwhelmed by emotions and confusion he didn't know what to think or do. I stood up and brought the dishes into the kitchen. Not bothering to wash them, I went back into the living room and took the papers out of his hands from where he had picked them up again.

"Come on," I said.

"What?" he asked.

"Come on," I said again, tugging on his hands. "You need some rest."

I brought him into the bedroom and helped him strip down to nothing but his boxers. I got down to my bra and panties, and we crawled into bed. He curled onto his side, and I wrapped around him. There was far too much of him for me to wrap around completely, but I did my best to surround him and pressed a kiss to his back. I would hold him tight for as long as he needed me.

24

GREG

Just like after my crash, when the family was so understanding and did everything they could to help me, I was indescribably grateful for the Freemans over the next two days. My mother hadn't gone into any details with Gus when she got to the complex. Instead, she just told him that there was an emergency in the family, and I needed to tend to it.

It left me with the decision of how much to tell them. I really had no reason to hold back from them. They were the closest thing to family I had outside of my mother and had been there for me from the first day I started working for them. I wanted them to know what I was going through and why I'd ended up walking off the compound so suddenly in the middle of the workday.

They already had a hint that my family life wasn't the best growing up. I didn't tell them the full story of everything that had happened because I didn't want to dwell on it. The whole point of moving out of Shelby was to escape that misery and find my own life. Of course, I had no idea I was actually moving right toward what I was trying to escape all along.

Now it was time to completely open up to the Freemans and let them know what had brought me to Charlotte in the first place. As soon as I did, they closed ranks around me. I felt their support and their love, and not for a second did I feel judged or looked down on.

They told me to take as much time as I needed away from work. When they first said it, I had no intention of actually doing it. Freeman Racing was my home. It was where I felt comfortable and happy. I was able to distract myself and immerse myself completely in what I had discovered was my favorite thing. But by that evening, I knew I wasn't going to be in any shape to go to work until the will was read.

I couldn't think straight. I couldn't get my brain to fully wrap around the situation and come to terms with the fact that this was reality.

Finally, the day came for the reading of the will. Now that Maya was sleeping in my bed every night, the second bedroom was legitimately a guest room, which meant Mom could stay with us rather than having to find a hotel. She was already going through enough. I didn't want her to have to be alone.

She was delighted to see Maya again. It seemed seeing her gave my mom some comfort as well. She always knew how important our friendship was to me and often asked about Maya. Seeing us not just back together geographically but finally actually together, did her heart good.

The morning of the will reading, Maya got up early and made us all breakfast. The tower of perfect, golden French toast in the middle of the table looked beautiful, but none of us seemed to have much of an appetite. We brewed cup after cup of coffee and sat around the table in anxious silence. I managed to get down a few bites of food, and Maya did the same before we finally gave up and went to get dressed.

We arrived at the lawyer's office a few minutes early, and the secretary directed us to the waiting area. It was empty, but not for long. Just a few moments after we arrived, three other women walked in. My mother immediately stiffened, and I knew that meant they were my father's family.

I'd never met my grandmother or my father's two sisters. Even when I was very young and he was still the strong, fun father I remembered back then, we never got together with his family. He always gave excuses that they lived far away, or they didn't like to travel. It seemed strange to me considering I had friends whose grandmothers lived on the other side of the country and came to visit, but it was considered a nonnegotiable conversation.

Now looking at my grandmother for the first time, I was beginning to understand what he might have been keeping us from. She looked at my mother with steel in her eyes and turned just as much darkness toward me.

"I can't believe you're here," she said through gritted teeth. "How could you be so selfish?"

"I'm not being selfish," my mother said. "This is Walter's will, not mine. I had nothing to do with it. If he wanted to leave something for his son, then that was his choice."

"It's ridiculous that you think either one of you is entitled to anything of his. You weren't good enough for him from the beginning. He never should have married you. You know the only reason he did it because he got you pregnant," my grandmother growled.

I could feel Maya's hand tighten around mine. She wanted to say something, but she was staying quiet. She didn't want to escalate anything or make this more challenging than it already was.

"That's what this is all about, isn't it?" Mom asked. "You hated that he married me. You hated that he stayed after Greg was born. You drove him away."

"I didn't do anything," my grandmother said. "He made that choice."

"No," Mom said. "He wrote me a letter. I know exactly what you did."

I looked over at her. "What do you mean?"

"Not now," Mom said. "She'll know soon enough."

Just then, the lawyer stepped out into the waiting room and called us back into the office. I chose a chair for Mom and made sure Maya and I bookended her so we could both hold her hands. There was no need for her to be exposed to my father's awful family.

I always grappled with the reality that my father just ran. He chose not to find a way to make himself better, but that he just abandoned us. Now that I was experiencing his family, I was starting to think it was less that he ran away and more that they dragged him away. These women clearly thought nothing of my mother or of me. And even though I had mixed feelings about my father, this experience was terrible.

The lawyer sat down and pulled a file out of his drawer. My grandmother immediately held up a hand.

"Before you even start, I want to make it extremely clear that I have no intention of accepting the terms of Walter's will."

"Are you saying you are going to contest the will?" the lawyer asked.

"Absolutely," my grandmother said. "My son ended his marriage to this woman many years ago. There was never a true relationship between them, anyway."

"How could you possibly say that?" my mother asked. "You were never around. You never interacted with me or saw us together."

"I didn't need to," my grandmother said. "I am well aware of the type of person you are. You manipulated my son into sleeping with you, and you tried to trap him by getting pregnant. You pushed him over the edge."

"I did nothing, but take care of him. The fact that he fell into alcoholism wasn't my fault. Trust me, he told me all about his father and your tendency to disappear from the world with a good Jack Daniels or two or ten," my mom said.

My grandmother gasped, her hands clutching the sides of the chair, and she looked like she was going to get up and launch at my mother.

"How dare you speak to her that way?" one of my father's sisters demanded.

"Stop it, Gladys," Mom said. "I don't want to hear anything from you. You have no right to be here."

My mother's voice was shaking slightly, and she held my hand tighter and tighter as she spoke. I could tell she was getting overwhelmed, but she was finally saying things she had been holding inside her for so long. Things I had no idea she lived with every day.

"I have far more right to be here than you do," the skeletally thin woman said acidly. "And far more than her, too."

Her sharp nod toward Maya made my muscles tense and protectiveness rush up inside me.

"Leave her out of this," I said.

"I think the best thing for everyone would be if we

proceeded," the lawyer said. "I hear your desire to contest the will because your son's decision to leave money to both his son and his ex-wife, but there are extenuating circumstances involved."

"What does that mean?" my grandmother asked.

"The letter he sent me," my mother said. "It was in the papers you gave to me."

"Excuse me?" my grandmother asked, sounding shocked that she had any part in getting communication from my father to my mother.

"Walter wrote letters to be included with his will," the lawyer explained.

"And mine detailed how you drove him into the worst of his drinking, then when he hit rock bottom and decided to seek treatment, you manipulated him into never coming back. I won't get into the grisly details right now, but I'll leave it at I know everything," Mom said.

My father's mother's face went pale. She knew exactly what Mom was talking about even if none of the rest of us did.

"Furthermore, Walter had an idea that you might attempt to stand in the way of his ex-wife and son getting the money he left for them as well as the life insurance. He left me a note to read if that was the case."

He reached into the file and brought out a piece of paper.

"Mom, leave it. I missed my son's whole life because of you. I regret every day leaving him behind."

"Walter," Mom whispered, the note in her voice something I hadn't heard since I was a little boy and things were still good.

"He worked extremely hard to build his company in the last couple of years and to invest well. He was very successful and wanted the family he felt he lost to be the beneficiaries of that. There are some items he left to you and to your daughters, but there is a clause in the will that states if you attempt to contest the will in any way, you are no longer eligible to receive anything," the lawyer said.

I didn't cry, but I was closer than I had been in a long time. There was still so much I didn't know about my father, but for the first time ever, I felt like I might get the answers I needed. The lawyer read my father's will, and as my grandmother and aunts stormed out of the office in a huff, my mother and I filled out the paperwork to start the process of receiving what he had left for us.

When we walked out of the office, I was a millionaire. Pending bank transfer, of course. Even just the thought of it was mind-blowing. We got back to the apartment, and Mom stepped into my room.

"I hope you don't take this wrong," she said, "because I appreciate you having me here very much. But I think I need some time to myself. I'm going to go get a hotel room for a few days before heading back home. My boss gave me bereavement leave so I have a little bit longer to process everything."

"I completely understand," I said, gathering her in a hug. "You know I'm here if you need me. Both of us are."

"I do," she said. "Thank you."

"And we'll get together for lunch before you go so we can talk about all this," I said.

She agreed and went to the bedroom to pack up. Maya and I said goodbye to her, and when the door closed, I held her close. It felt good to be home, and to be alone with her.

MAYA

"How does Thai food sound?" Greg asked, coming into the room with a handful of takeout menus. "Or we could do Indian again. That was really good."

"I'm up for anything," I said. "Thai sounds really good, though. Some peanut noodles would be amazing. And some of those spring rolls. Oh, and you know that stuff that is the broccoli and it has that brown sauce on it, and they serve it with rice? I want some of that, too."

Greg laughed as he sat down on the couch next to me and opened the menu. "I guess you don't need to see the menu, huh?"

"Well, I might," I said. "I haven't had it memorized or anything. Maybe there's something else on there that I want to try."

I scooted even closer to him and looked over his shoulder at the menu. It was one of those rare nights when I didn't feel like cooking. But Greg never complained about that. On some of those nights, he would jump in and cook dinner for us. And on others, both of us decided to be lazy and indulge ourselves with some takeout. That was one of those nights.

It was Thursday, so I had the night off. That meant I wanted to just lounge around the house with him and enjoy some time together. It'd been two weeks since we sat in the lawyer's office and the huge shock of finding out about his father's legacy being left to him.

In those two weeks, something had shifted. It wasn't a massive change, and it definitely wasn't negative. A lot of people who discovered they were suddenly wealthy would have changed completely. But not Greg. There wasn't even the slightest hint of being a rich, snobby ass. He was still going to work every day and putting every bit of himself into his career.

He had another race and pushed just as much as he always did. It was like the money hadn't even registered to him yet.

Or it had and he was determined to not let it change him.

I loved that about him. When I found out just how much money he was inheriting from his father, I worried he might let it get to him. After so many years of having almost nothing, it would make sense that he would get wrapped up in it. It would have been a completely normal response for him to get a big head and want to just start splashing money around because it was suddenly there. He might have even started acting like a jerk and looking down on people.

But I should have known Greg better than that. He didn't let any of it affect him that way. He just wasn't that type of person. Instead, the shift was between us. And it couldn't have been better.

All of a sudden, we were completely domesticated. We never said anything about it or had any big talk about it. It just was the way it was. We had already been sharing a bed before his mother came to town and stayed at the apartment for those few days, but it never went back. His room became our room.

And it wasn't just our sleeping arrangements that showed we were very much settled into our new relationship status. All of our free time was spent together. Anytime we needed to do anything like go grocery shopping or running errands for the apartment, we were there together.

The fact that we never talked about it only made it feel more real. Like we didn't need to clarify anything because it was so obvious both of us already knew and were blissfully happy with it. There was nothing strange about it, nothing we had to get used to. This felt like the way everything always should have been between us.

When I pointed out a couple more things on the menu, Greg looked at me and laughed.

"Have you forgotten to eat over the last couple of days or something?" he asked.

"You know I haven't. Considering you make me lunch, you know I have at least one meal a day. Everything just looks delicious. I thought we could share a lot of these," I said.

He shrugged. "They do sound good."

It took a while after Greg called the restaurant for our food to be delivered, and by the time it got there, I was famished. I cleared off the coffee table and spread all of the takeout containers in front of us. Handing Greg chopsticks, I dug in.

We stayed up eating and cuddling on the couch, watching all the episodes of TV shows we saved throughout the week so we could watch them together. As it got later, Greg got tired and had to go to bed so he could get up for work in the morning. I stayed up a little bit longer, which was usual for me. I didn't want to throw off my schedule too much and be exhausted at work.

It seemed I stayed up a little too late that night, because the next morning I was exhausted and could barely open my eyes when Greg woke me up to kiss me goodbye. I immediately fell back to sleep, but that didn't last long. Less than an hour later, a sudden wave of nausea hit me and woke me out of a deep sleep.

I scrambled out of bed and rushed into the bathroom, just making it in time before I threw up. I stayed there on the bathroom floor for several minutes until the sickness calmed down enough for me to brush my teeth and splash cold water on my face. Seconds later, another wave hit me, and I was back on the floor.

It was another half an hour before I managed to crawl back into bed and grab my phone. I sent Greg a text warning him that I was sick, and it probably came from the takeout the night before. Since we had eaten many of the same things, I wanted to give him a heads-up before it hit him. I didn't want to have to call out of work, so I set my alarm and closed my eyes for just a little while longer.

When I woke up, my stomach was still feeling uneasy, but I didn't get sick again. I went into the bathroom and took a big dose of Pepto to try to ward off any more incidents. Just to be safe, I called the Thai restaurant and let them know I had gotten sick after eating their food.

They apologized profusely, but I reassured them I would be just fine. I just wanted to let them know in case they heard from anybody else. When I got off the phone, I took another quick dose of Pepto and got dressed for work.

As soon as I got to the bar, I walked right up to Lindsey and asked her for a ginger ale.

She looked at me strangely as she poured it. "Are you okay?"

"I'm fine," I told her. "Greg and I just had a major Thai food extravaganza last night, and I don't think it's sitting with me right. I got some indigestion last night and ended up staying up pretty late so that I could sit up, but it just really hit me this morning. I'm feeling much better than I did, though."

"So, you're not sick?" she asked.

I laughed. "No. I'm not going to infect any of your customers."

I took a long sip of the ginger ale and let out a sigh. It was so delicious and immediately helped to make me feel better.

"How's everything else?" she asked. "How's Greg dealing with everything?"

"Pretty well. I mean, there're obviously still moments when it hits him, and he goes through a lot of emotions. I think he's still trying to figure out exactly how he feels about everything. He and his mom went to lunch and talked through things. He learned a lot about his dad and his family. I think it helped him kind of process a lot of things that went on when he was younger," I said.

"That's good," she said. "It's just so crazy he was here in Charlotte this entire time and nobody knew. Do you think it's possible he knew Greg was in town?"

"I think he probably did," I said. "A man who felt bad enough to leave that much money to his son and leave a note like that for his mother wouldn't just have that spontaneously come up in his life. He thought about Greg for a long time. He would have tried to find him. I wouldn't even be surprised to find out he knew Greg was racing and came to see some of the races."

"I hope he did," Lindsey said. "I know he did a lot of really horrible things, but at the same time, it's obvious he loved him. It would be nice to know he could see that his son grew up to be a good man. And in a way would actually be getting back at him, too. He would be able to see that Greg succeeded even without him being there. That he didn't destroy him."

It wasn't a plan I had thought all the way through, but suddenly I knew this was the right moment. The moment I had been waiting for it since the first night I started working for her. I gathered up all my courage, took another sip of ginger ale, and looked her right in the eyes.

"Speaking of success," I said. "I wanted to talk to you about my job."

She looked briefly concerned. "You're not going to tell me that now that Greg has money, you're going to quit and just go be a pampered kept woman, are you?"

I had to laugh at that. It was just so detailed and specific.

"Yes," I said sarcastically. "Just like you. No, that's not what I'm doing. What I wanted to talk to you about is moving up from my scrub spot. You mentioned I would be able to climb up through the ranks, and I think that I've proven myself. But, if I haven't, I'd like to talk to you about what milestones I would need to hit in order for you to think I would be ready to move up."

She grinned. "I don't think anybody has ever spoken that professionally in this bar ever in its existence. But, yes, of course you've proven yourself. You are extremely valuable here, and I had already started thinking about progressing you up a bit."

"Really?"

"Absolutely. Now, I told you I'm thinking about expanding and opening a restaurant."

"Yes," I said. "You were thinking about taking over the building next door."

"Exactly. But before we are going to be able to do that, I wanted to test out some of the ideas. I would really like to restyle the menu here at the bar and try to find items to be the first ones on the restaurant when we open. I would really like good, fresh food. Not as much fried stuff. We already have the best burgers in town, but I want more. So, I wanted to see if you would like to be involved in something like that," she said.

"How?" I asked, getting excited but not wanting to build myself up too much.

"I've tried your cooking. You're really fantastic. And I've heard that your baking skills are getting better all the time. So, I'd like you to have a hand in building the menu. Be sort of a sous chef. I'd still need your help with other elements of running the kitchen. You would probably still act as a barback and support the servers until everything gets up and running. But I want you helping out on the line more and bringing some of your recipes to the menu."

I wished that it was a moment when I could be sophisticated and eloquent. I should have come up with something meaningful to say, something that would reassure her I was a good choice and wouldn't let her down. Instead, I broke into tears.

Lindsey laughed and came around the bar to hug me.

26

GREG

The race that weekend was at a track a couple of hours away, so we were leaving just after lunch on Saturday. It was a night race, so we wouldn't be finishing up until late, and then we were going to get hotel rooms to stay the night rather than trying to get home. It meant I had to go an entire night without Maya, and I really didn't like that idea.

I had gotten very accustomed to her being in my space. And that was something I had never said about a woman before. And if somebody else said something like that, I probably would have thought it was a bad thing. It sounded boring, like she was just kind of there and I was used to it.

In all honesty, this was far from the reality. Being accustomed to Maya being a part of every aspect of my life was better than anything I ever could have imagined. It wasn't that I was just used to her. It was that I had fully knitted her into my daily existence and didn't like having to be without her. I wasn't looking forward to not spending Saturday night curled up around her, so I wanted to have as much time with her as I could before I left.

Before I went to work on Friday, I left her the usual

lunch and the sticky note attached to it which told her to wake me up when she got in. I could easily sleep on the way to the race. Recently Quentin had invested in a team bus to use when we had races not at our local track.

Rather than using the smaller equipment trucks and traveling separately, we had workers from the complex bring the equipment in larger trailers and the team all traveled together in the bus. It wasn't just more comfortable. It was also a chance to talk and strategize.

But it also meant I got to steal some extra time with Maya when she came home from work. Even if I was tired, I looked forward to those late-night interludes.

She ended up getting home earlier than I anticipated that Saturday morning. Usually Friday nights were so busy it was almost four by the time she dragged herself into the bedroom and collapsed in the sheets beside me. But that night, it was only around 2:00 a.m. when she made it back.

She slipped into bed beside me and wrapped her arms around my waist. Her cold hands pressed to my chest, breaking through any lingering sleep that might have been there. I turned over my shoulder and kissed her.

"How was your night at work?" I asked. "You're home early. Is everything okay?"

"Everything's great," she said. "It just wasn't that busy of a night. We were able to get through all the closing things faster than we usually do. Guess what?"

"What?" I asked, rolling onto my back so I could wrap my arm around her.

She pulled up to rest on my chest and look down into my face.

"Lindsey is giving me a promotion."

"A promotion?" I asked. "What kind of promotion?"

"Well, now she wants me to help out the cooks more.

She's planning on expanding out and opening a restaurant sometime soon. And she wants to rework the menu at the bar and find out the kinds of food people would want to order before she does it. So, she wants me to help the cooks, and may even want to use some of my recipes," Maya said.

"That's amazing," I said, rising up to kiss her. "I'm proud of you."

"Thank you," she said. "I'm really excited. She even mentioned my baking, which might mean I'll get to make some desserts if I can really get my scales down."

"I will happily try anything you have to offer."

"Oh, really?" she asked.

Her head dipped down and caught my lips in another kiss. I held her close, slipping my tongue into her mouth. The talk started to turn to a celebration, and I was just about to roll her onto her back when Maya suddenly pulled back from the kiss. She paused, then pushed my chest to move away from me. Her eyes widened, and she jumped out of bed.

Scurrying to the bathroom, she pushed the door closed, but it didn't latch. I heard her getting sick, and I cringed. I had hoped she would be better by now. I had never gotten sick even after she warned me that she thought it was the Thai food that got to her.

Worried, I got out of bed and followed her into the bathroom. She was kneeling on the floor, her arms crossed on the toilet seat and her forehead rested against it. I sat down on the edge of the tub, and she looked up at me, then groaned.

"You shouldn't be in here," she said. "I don't want you seeing me like this."

"I've seen you like this before," I said. A lot of times.

"Yeah, but that was different. That was before we were... like we are now."

I laughed and shook my head at her. "That doesn't change anything. You're still my best friend. I didn't suddenly stop being willing to take care of you when I manned up and realized my feelings for you. If anything, I want to take care of you even more now."

She gave a faint smile and looked like she was going to say something, but another wave of sickness hit her, and her head dropped down into the toilet. I reached over and gathered her hair to hold it back for her. I used the other hand to gently rub her back until she was done.

When she was sure the waves of sickness were over, I helped her to her feet and supported her while she walked over to the sink. If there was one thing I remembered about her getting sick when we were younger, it was that she tended to get dizzy when she threw up.

She rinsed her mouth out, then brushed her teeth. I helped her back into the bedroom and held the blankets up for her while she slid into bed. I got in on my side and slid over to wrap my arms around her. I held her close and kissed her on the side of the neck.

"I'm getting worried about you," I said. "If you're not feeling better really soon, you should go to the doctor. There might be something else going on. I didn't even get sick, so I don't think it's food poisoning."

"It could be," she said. "I did eat some things you didn't. And some people are more sensitive to foodborne pathogens than other people."

I looked at her strangely, and she let out a sigh.

"I was starting to wonder about it, so I did some research. They say it's not uncommon for foodborne illness to not hit until several hours or even a couple of days after eating, and then it can last up to a week. It probably came from one of the things I ate that you didn't, or you are just resistant to it," she said.

"You should still talk to somebody," I said. "I don't want you to be sick and just suffering when they might be able to give you medicine or something."

"I'm going to try to ride it out for at least a little another day or two," she said. "I hate going to the doctor, especially if it's not for something they can give me medicine for. Which they wouldn't be able to if it was food poisoning and might not be able to if it's a sickness like the stomach flu. Besides, don't forget that I haven't been able to get insurance yet. I had it through the Cabinet Factory, but obviously that's gone," she said.

"I wouldn't worry about the insurance," I said. "I'm a millionaire now, remember? I think I can cover a couple of doctors' bills for you."

She giggled, and I kissed her on the tip of the nose. We nuzzled down into the pillows and went to sleep. I had already packed everything I would need for the race, so I stayed in bed with Maya for as long as I possibly could Saturday morning. When it was time that I finally had to leave, I gently kissed her and whispered goodbye, then grabbed my bag and headed out.

The lack of sleep got to me almost as soon as I got onto the bus. I put a sleep mask over my eyes, put my earbuds in, and went to sleep. I got a decent nap in, and then when I woke up, I moved over to sit next to Minnie. She was deeply engrossed in a paperback, but she put it down beside her when I sat down.

"Hi, Greg," she said in the gentle, nurturing way that always made me feel like even if something was going bad in the world, she could make it better. It was the tone of a woman who was made to be a grandmother and would have just filled in with anybody around her if the babies hadn't been born. "How are you?"

"I'm doing fine," I said. "But I think Maya might be sick. And she was talking to me about the fact that she doesn't have insurance. Obviously, Lindsey doesn't provide insurance to people working in the bar, and she doesn't have the policy she used to. I wanted to know if there was a way I could get her put on my insurance."

"She's sick?" Minnie asked. "I hope nothing serious."

"No," I said, shaking my head. "I don't think so. I think she just has a little bit of a bug. But if it is something else, or if something might go wrong at some point, I want to make sure she can go to the doctor. Is there a way she can be added to my policy?"

The Freeman matriarch looked at me with a knowing expression, but I didn't say anything else. Right now, I was going on what Maya told me, and that was that she was dealing with some food poisoning. And if that wasn't the case, then she might have picked up a stomach virus. I just wanted to make sure she got the care she needed. No matter what was happening.

27

MAYA

Sunday was my second day off during the week because the bar was closed, and usually I spent it with Greg. When he'd first mentioned the race and that he was going to be gone not just most of the day Saturday, but all day Sunday as well because of an event the day after the race, I was disappointed. I would miss him and wished I could go along even though I knew I needed to be at the bar Saturday night.

But when I woke up that Sunday, I was glad I hadn't gone. I still felt horrible and didn't want to do anything but lie in bed for the rest of the day.

Hopefully just being a bit of a slug for the day would help me get over whatever was going on so I could go back to normal. To say that I wasn't great at being sick was a major understatement. I didn't get sick often, and usually when I did, it was fairly minor. It had actually been years since I was sick enough to actually throw up, and I just wasn't handling it well.

I hated being sick. And even more than that, I hated Greg seeing me sick. It was ridiculous, especially considering he had already said it didn't bother him in the least and he wanted to take care of me, but there was still embarrassment. He talked about taking care of me when we were younger and I was sick, but that was just the thing. We were younger. Much younger.

At that point, he was still just Greg, my best friend. He was the only person in the world who I could rely on and really trust to take care of me. There were a lot of times when I felt like he was the only person in the world who cared about me at all. Who loved me. If it was going to be anybody who was going to take care of me when I was sick, it was going to be him.

Things were different now. Not only were we adults, but our relationship had totally changed. There was something very different about him holding my hair for me and rubbing my back twenty seconds after I was getting ready to peel his boxers off.

I needed to get over it. If we were going to have a serious relationship, I needed to accept him seeing me at my worst. And this was my worst.

I just wanted to stay in my pajamas, drink an Olympic swimming pool's worth of ginger ale, and get over this. Greg didn't have a TV in his bedroom, but I was comfortable and wanted to stay there. It was also closer to a bathroom than the living room couch, and I wasn't going to discount the value of that. Not when the waves of nausea were coming so randomly and suddenly.

Instead, I just pulled my laptop up onto the bed with me and was watching a stream of crappy reality TV. I wanted something mindless that I didn't have to think too much about and that would be okay to miss if I fell asleep. In fact, it would be fantastic if I fell asleep.

Before I could nod off, though, a particular scene of the

episode jumped out at me. I sat up a little straighter, my breath stopping in my throat. I rewound the episode and watched the scene again. I listened carefully to how the woman was describing how she felt and the reaction of her best friend. It took one more watch through for me to really understand what I was seeing. And what I was realizing.

I got out of bed and dragged on clothes, not caring if they were clean or what I looked like. This was not the time for me to be concerned with vanity. I needed to get to the pharmacy and back home as fast as I could.

It only took a few minutes for me to get to the store and back. I was shaking and exhausted when I got into the bathroom, and I realized I hadn't eaten a real meal in two days. But right then, that was the least of my concerns. I flipped the plastic bag over, dumping all the cardboard boxes of pregnancy tests out onto the bathroom floor. I had gotten one of every brand and type I could find.

I didn't want any sort of ambiguity. I needed results, and to be sure they were accurate.

After taking several of the tests, I lined them up on the counter and set the alarm on my phone. It didn't seem like waiting three minutes could be so much of a challenge, but those were the longest three minutes of my life.

The minutes ticked by painfully slowly, and I checked my phone over and over to make sure I hadn't missed the timer going off. I forced myself to go into the kitchen and raid the cabinet to see if I could find something easy to eat. I had just pulled a can of soup out of the cabinet when my phone alerted me that it was time. Setting the can down, I walked slowly back to the bathroom.

For all that waiting and anticipation, now I was hesitant to see the results. Just like I had been before Greg and I settled into our relationship, I was in a place where so many things were possible. And as long as I hadn't seen those results, they were all still possible. I knew as soon as I saw the results, things were going to change.

Even if it was negative, having this experience forced me to think about the future in a totally new way. A way I hadn't before, and one I didn't know if I was ready to even consider.

But it wasn't something I could think about. Because the tests weren't negative. I looked at every one of them. I picked up each and looked at the results, comparing it to the box to make sure I was reading it correctly. But every single one of them said the same thing. I was pregnant.

I sat down on the edge of the tub and stared at the sticks in my hand. I didn't cry. Instead, I tried as hard as I could to think logically. Letting myself get overwhelmed and overemotional right now wasn't going to do any good. I needed to approach this in the calmest way possible. I needed to keep a clear head and think it through.

The most important thing I needed to figure out was what I wanted to do. It was a massive, insurmountable question. This wasn't just one decision that loomed over me heavily. No matter what choice I made, I wasn't just making that one choice. I was deciding something that would affect the rest of my life. In that one choice, I was making countless others.

For the first time in a long time, I longed for my mother. I wished I had her to call and talk about this with so I could hear her advice and get her comfort. I needed someone to talk this out with, but I didn't have my mother. I didn't have a family. I didn't have anyone except the people I met here.

And Greg.

Thinking about him made my stomach sink. This really wasn't just about me. It never was. This was about Greg, too, and I had no idea what that meant. Children weren't something we ever talked about. Of course it wasn't. Why would we? We hadn't even ever really talked about being together.

This whole time I convinced myself that the fact that we hadn't sat down for that monumental conversation was a good thing. It meant it was natural. It was just what it was supposed to be between us.

Now I was wondering if it actually meant our relationship was up in the air. A pregnancy wasn't supposed to be in the cards for us. Not right at this point, at least. I had no idea how Greg was going to react to the prospect of being a father.

It occurred to me right then that even having that thought was a big deal. It meant whether I realized it or not, I had decided how I felt about it. I didn't need to think about it anymore or consider any options. There weren't really any options but one. I was going to have a baby. I was going to be a mother.

It was mind-blowing. Even as I sat there staring at the test and telling myself over and over that it was real, I didn't feel like I was really grasping the magnitude of it. There was no way I could tell Greg about it right then. I needed a little bit of time.

Fortunately, I had it. The media event was a fairly last-minute addition to the race weekend, tacked on because they were already planning on spending the night on Saturday. This meant Greg would be at the track for the better part of the late morning and early afternoon. Then the team would need to load up all the equipment and set off on the ride home, which would take a couple more hours.

They would most likely go to the compound and unload all the equipment so it didn't need to be done on Monday, which would push them into the evening. If I knew the Freemans at all, I knew they would probably then all have dinner together. All that added up to him not getting home until late that night.

It gave me the time I needed to keep resting and keep thinking this through. At the same time, I didn't want him to think I was completely ignoring him. I stuffed all the pregnancy tests into the cardboard boxes, put those into the bag from the pharmacy, and buried them in the bottom of the trash can.

Climbing back into bed, I changed the show on my laptop. I checked the time and realized he would probably be busy, which meant it was the perfect time for me to text him.

If he was busy when I messaged him, he wouldn't be able to respond immediately, which meant I wouldn't break and tell him about the pregnancy right then. And that would have been terrible. This way he would see the message when he had some time and know I was thinking about him.

The message sent, I curled up under the blankets, stuffed my head under the pillow, and did my best not to cry.

28

GREG

The popularity of Merry's events never ceased to amaze me. Even when she came up with something on the fly and put it together at the very last minute, it seemed to be a tremendous success.

The media event she put together for the day after the race wasn't a completely new idea. It was something she had done a few times before, so at least she had the basic structure she could build off of. However, it was still a matter of piecing together the vendors, media, and other elements to bring it together on incredibly short notice.

Despite that, the crowd was huge. Fans swarmed to the parking lot she had set up, hoping for a chance to meet Darren and me. It was very much like the tailgate parties we had at home but felt more intimate because of the smaller scale, and it wasn't right before a race, so we had more time to linger.

Just like she coached us, we ignored the media and put all of our focus on the fans. After all, they were the reason we were there. If it wasn't for the people who loved to watch us race and had a loyalty to our team, we wouldn't matter. So, Darren and I spent the event greeting fans, taking pictures, and signing autographs.

It really was fun. I enjoyed seeing people's faces light up when they got near us and felt humbled when they talked about how devoted they were to our team. It was a good reminder of why we worked so hard, and why I was determined not to let the money I inherited stop me from racing. I wasn't going to let it change me. It was just a nice cushion if I needed it.

The event was fantastic, but it did mean we got back on the road to Charlotte late in the afternoon. By the time we unloaded everything at the complex and had dinner, it was well into the night. It wasn't nearly as late as it usually was when Maya came home from the bar, so I was surprised when I got back to the apartment and didn't find her up.

I had expected to find her in the kitchen coming up with new, amazing recipes, or battling against the baked goods she hadn't quite gotten to her standards yet. As I approached, I wondered what kind of music she would be listening to and looked forward to her silly dancing.

But when I opened the door, the apartment was dark and quiet. Was it possible she had gone out?

I stopped by the kitchen to put some leftovers in the refrigerator, then went to the bedroom. Maya curled up asleep came as a surprise. It wasn't the light, shallow sleep of someone who was watching TV or reading a book and drifted off. This was deep, full sleep with the lights off and the blankets pulled up close around her face.

I worried that she might still not be feeling well. I was totally convinced at that point it had nothing to do with food poisoning. She was grappling with something else, and she couldn't just keep ignoring it. I decided the next day I was going to make sure she went to the doctor. Even if I had to call and make the appointment myself.

It would make her feel much better to know Minnie was going to look into having Maya added to my insurance so she wouldn't have another situation where she didn't feel like she couldn't go to the doctor. Minnie said she wasn't completely sure of all the details and would have to run it by Vince but was certain they could work it out by listing her as my domestic partner.

That kind of left a bad taste in my mouth. I wasn't sure why, but it didn't sound right. There was an almost judgmental lean to that, and it seemed like less than we actually were. That was a ridiculous reaction, I knew, but I couldn't help it. At least it would make sure she had insurance fast and would be able to get the care she needed when she needed it.

And until it went through, I would be able to pay for her care. I just hoped when she finally did get seen, it wasn't anything serious.

I leaned down and gently kissed her temple, brushing away some strands of hair that hung across her face. I couldn't help but stand there and watch her sleep for a few seconds. She was so beautiful, even with no makeup, her hair a mess from lying in bed.

I went into the bathroom as quietly as I could, so I didn't wake her up. Carefully turning on the shower, I stepped under the hot water and let it rinse away the day. I stepped out, still trying to be quiet and not disturb her. But I promptly kicked the trash can, sending it tumbling to the tile floor and skittering toward the wall.

Cursing under my breath, I stood absolutely still, listening to see if I would hear Maya stirring in the bedroom. I didn't hear anything, so I leaned down to clean up the mess. Picking up the trash can, I stood it up right again, then went to work picking up all the trash that had spilled out and spread across the floor. Among the tissues, Q-tips, makeup removal pads, and empty shampoo containers, I noticed a plastic bag from the pharmacy.

It struck me as strange, and when I picked it up, I noticed it had several things in it. Concerned it might have accidentally fallen into the trash can from the counter, I undid the loose knot at the top and looked inside. My heart jumped into my throat.

The bag was full of pregnancy tests. Every box in that bag was open and a used test was inside. I sat down hard at the edge of the tub, the bag slipping from my fingers. Gathering myself, I reached in and took out one of the tests. The results were no longer legible. The test had been taken too long before for the results to still be visible and accurate.

But that didn't change that the tests were there. A bag full of used pregnancy tests in the bathroom I was sharing with Maya. I stuffed the test back into the box where I had gotten it, tied the bag closed again, and buried it at the bottom of the trash can where it had been before I managed to kick it over.

Still sitting at the edge of the tub, not wanting to move, I thought back to our first time together. It was a surprise, not something we had carefully planned out. Maya was so busy getting my clothes off I hadn't been able to think clearly. And that meant I hadn't grabbed a condom.

Come to think of it, I probably didn't even have one at the time. It wasn't like I was running around having a ton of sex. There was no reason for me to keep condoms stocked in the apartment. I bought a box after that first time, but we definitely didn't use them our first night together.

I hadn't even been thinking about it. We used a condom

every other time since, as far as I could recall, so I must have just let that first oversight slide out of my memory.

And it was a major oversight. Possibly one with huge consequences. What if Maya was pregnant? What would that mean for us?

It would be a lie if I said that thought hadn't flickered through my mind when she was talking about feeling sick. Then the look on Minnie's face when I was talking about getting her on my insurance led me in that direction as well. But it hadn't been a serious contemplation. It was just one of those things that briefly flashed into my thoughts, then left.

After all, she was convinced she had food poisoning. The more logical thing after that was that she was dealing with a stomach virus. It didn't seem plausible that she could actually be carrying my baby.

I thought of all the nights of hard work she had put in since that first time. She had pushed herself, working hard for long hours. That couldn't be good for her or for the baby. Not to mention the alcohol she had right around that time. I knew she wasn't drinking now because she didn't want to drink while she was at work, but I was still getting worried.

I decided right then I wasn't going to bring it up to her. Even though a big part of me wanted to wake her up and demand she give me an explanation, I decided to stay quiet. I wouldn't say I found the tests or give any indication I knew what was going on. I was going to wait for her to bring it up when the time was right for her.

The truth was, if I was freaking out about this, she definitely was.

I couldn't even begin to imagine what it must be like to think about carrying a new life inside her. That she was the only thing supporting it and taking care of it. She must have been in a strange place trying to figure out how she felt and what was going to happen moving forward. I would give her the respect of deciding when to broach the topic with me.

Feeling a little better, I went into the bedroom and slid into bed beside her. I reached one arm around her and pulled Maya in close to my side. She sighed and rested her head on my chest, draping her arm over my stomach. I kissed the top of her head and closed my eyes, envisioning a baby that had her eyes and my hair.

29

MAYA

When I woke up Monday morning, I braced myself for another wave of horrible nausea. I lay on my back for a few seconds, just waiting to have to run to the bathroom. When it didn't immediately hit, I cautiously pulled myself up to a sitting position and waited again.

It was far earlier in the morning than I really needed to be up, but there was so much on my mind, I couldn't sleep. Greg lay there beside me, deeply asleep and unaffected by me moving. I didn't even notice him come in the night before. By the time I went to sleep, I was so exhausted and overwhelmed I was completely dead to the world. I didn't even realize he had gotten home until I came awake for a few seconds in the middle of the night and noticed he was there beside me.

I could feel his warmth and his arm wrapped around me. I nuzzled against him, wanting to enjoy that feeling. Easing out of bed, I made my way into the kitchen to make him breakfast. As long as I could move around and not get sick again, I wanted to do something special for him.

After all, he was about to get some news that would

change his life. I wanted to give him at least a little bit of pampering before that.

As I cooked, my stomach started to feel a little bit squishy. Not exactly sick, like I needed to rush off the bathroom and throw up again, but just unsure of itself. I had heard of women who didn't really experience morning sickness when they were pregnant. Instead, they experienced nausea later in the day, or kind of on a perpetual basis, just dealing with different degrees of it at any given time.

It seemed I was going to be that type of woman. At least, that was what I was getting from the last few days of being sick. One more thing I was going to have to think about, one more thing that was completely new to me and that I would need to wrap my head around as I dealt with it for the months ahead.

At least I wouldn't have to do it completely alone. I needed to tell Greg and just accept however he was going to react to it. It was the right thing to do. He needed to know, and I needed to not be on my own through this.

So, I was going to make him breakfast, and we would sit down and have a conversation before he went to work. This would give him a built-in out. He would be able to leave without seeming like a jerk and spend the day at work thinking about the whole situation so he could figure out how he felt about it and be ready to talk about it when he got home.

This was my plan. I was studying it and felt good about it. Right up until Greg woke up.

I was expecting him to react to me making breakfast the same way he usually did. He would come into the kitchen, wrap his arms around my waist, and nuzzle his face down into that curve between my neck and shoulder. He would tell me whatever I was making smelled good and go over and get himself a cup of coffee. It was an easy, predictable rhythm we had fallen into and a good start to any day.

Except, apparently, that day. I was at the stove making a stack of banana walnut pancakes to go with the bacon frying up crisp on a griddle and the eggs I was going to scramble up last minute when I heard Greg coming down the hallway.

I readied myself, but he walked in and walked right past me. He went over to the coffee maker and poured himself a cup, barely even acknowledging that I was there. Just a quick glance out of the corner of his eye and nothing else.

"Good morning," I said.

"Morning," he said. "How are you?"

"I'm fine," I said. "Just thought I would make you breakfast before you went to work."

"That was nice of you," he said. "I appreciate it."

I nodded, and he walked out of the kitchen to the living room. He sat down and turned the news on. He continued to be weird through the rest of the morning and as we sat eating breakfast. I decided then not to tell him that morning. For all my bravado, with him already acting strange, I didn't want to venture into that.

A week later, Greg hadn't stopped being weird. Some moments when he was friendlier than others, I thought he might be going back to his usual self. He would wrap me up in a hug or kiss me, but he still didn't feel like him. He was being strange, pulling away from me. It felt like he had reconsidered what was going on between us.

Maybe he'd talked about it more with his mother, or after inheriting from his father he decided I was better left in his past. Or at least that he could do better now and wanted to reset our relationship. Maybe he was upset with me about something and just didn't want to say anything.

There were sometimes when I caught him looking at me and there was an expression in his eyes like I had done something wrong.

I couldn't think of anything, but he never started a conversation, so all I could do was wait and hope.

Maybe I wouldn't tell him. At least not yet. If we were going to end up breaking up, there was no point in opening up to him now. I didn't want to seem like I was trying to trap him the way his grandmother accused his mother of trapping his father. If this was going to be the way it was going to work out between us, I would wait until it all went down and figured out what I was going to do next.

As steady and secure as I tried to be, the situation got more painful and more challenging every day. I was still feeling sick, and I couldn't seem to get enough energy. After the home pregnancy test, I finally managed to get into my doctor for an appointment.

After confirming with a test in her office, she went over the timeline I gave her and the start of my last period, then gave me my due date. Part of me was excited. Just hearing the day when I could anticipate my baby being born was a thrill.

At the same time, I couldn't help but think about Greg. He should have been there with me. These were all things that we should be hearing together. Not because I couldn't handle it or because I couldn't make these decisions by myself, but because he was involved, and no matter what was going on, there was still a big part of me that wanted him to be there every single step of the way.

Not to mention how much my heart still ached for him. How much it killed me to think that what I thought was such an amazing start to our relationship could be over.

I left the doctor's office just before I had to head into

work. The emotion of it all crashed down on me as I drove toward the bar with the stack of papers and information stuffed in my glove compartment so no one would see them.

I didn't want to completely break down about it, but I couldn't seem to help myself. I walked into the bar fighting tears, trying to stay as strong as I possibly could. But the second I went into the back to clock in and saw Lindsey, I was a complete mess.

Bursting into tears, I hung my head and gave up even trying to hold it together and not be a total disaster. Lindsey put down the box of to-go containers she was putting in the storeroom right next to the monitor where I clocked in. Rushing over to me, she wrapped her arms around me and held me close.

"What's going on?" she asked. "What's wrong?"

"I think Greg is going to break up with me," I said with a sob. "It just started, and now I think it's all over."

Lindsey just kept hugging me while I clung to her and cried. She let me get it out until I was calm enough for her to step back and hold me by the shoulders while she looked me in the eye.

"Why do you think that?" she asked.

I shrugged, not ready to divulge the full story to her yet. "He's just being really weird. He's different. Like he's pulling away."

She shook her head. "I don't think he's going to break up with you. I'm just going to start right there. I think every-thing is going to be absolutely fine. But if something happens, I can promise you, you still have me."

"Really?"

"Of course. You think I would give up our friendship for some silly boy? Never. And because I know what you went through and what's probably on your mind right now, I want to show you something. Come with me," she said.

"Where are we going?"

"Just come with me," she said, taking my hand and leading me through a door at the back of the storage room I had never seen open before.

When she opened the door, I was shocked to see a short staircase leading up to another door. We climbed up to it, and she reached into her pocket for the keys. Unlocking the door, she opened it up and gestured for me to go inside.

"Go ahead," she said. "I promise it's safe."

I walked in, and she reached around to flip a light switch right next to the door. The overhead fixture illuminated a small living room, and ahead of me I could see a kitchen and a hallway.

"What is this?" I asked.

"When my grandfather first designed the building to have the bar in it, he wanted an apartment over it where he could live. This is before he married my grandmother. He lived here for a long time, even right after they got married before they bought their house. Then my father lived here before he met my mother. I have not lived here, but I've been known to take a nap on that couch every now and then."

"This is amazing. I had no idea it was here," I said.

"Most people don't. But I wanted to show you because I wanted you to know if something happens and you are suddenly out of Greg's apartment, you're not homeless. You absolutely have somewhere to go."

I looked at her with my eyes still dripping and my mouth hanging open. "You would let me stay here?"

"Absolutely. For as long as you wanted. And, silver lining, it would make your commute to work much easier."

I laughed, and she gave me another hug. It made me feel better, but there was still an ache in my heart. I threw everything into work, trying to focus as much as I could so I didn't dwell on Greg. When I got home the next morning, I went into my old bedroom and crawled into the empty, abandoned bed and fell asleep.

30

I didn't think I was going to find myself back in the place where I would be lying awake listening for Maya to come into the house after work and wondering if she would come to bed. I had just gotten so accustomed to her always coming in, there was no question. It wasn't even my room anymore. It was *our* room.

But that Monday, things changed. It had been tense and a bit awkward between us for the last week since I found out about the pregnancy tests. Every day, I waited for her to say something about it. Every day, I expected that conversation to start, especially when she gave me one of those looks like she was thinking hard and trying to come up with the exact words she wanted to say.

But she never did. Never once did she even come close to broaching the subject. A couple of times, I tried to lead her into it. I asked her how she was feeling, if her stomach was doing better. I asked if she had made an appointment with the doctor. I thought it might make it easier if she had a smooth and easy way to slip into the conversation.

Instead, she deftly avoided the topic and answered her way around the questions. She wasn't lying, but she definitely wasn't telling the truth, either. Maybe she did feel better than she did those first couple of days and there would have been no reason for her to talk to a doctor about food poisoning.

But I still wondered if she had gone to the doctor at all. And I expected her to take those questions and explain why she was feeling sick. When she didn't, an uncomfortable reality started to sink in. It wasn't something I even thought about it first. It didn't even occur to me.

It started creeping around somewhere in the back of my mind by Wednesday. But I pushed it down, swallowing it and forcing it away so that I didn't think about it. I didn't think much about it again until that weekend when she still hadn't said anything even all day on Thursday. Her day off would have been the perfect opportunity, time for us to spend together talking and working things out.

But it was Monday, a full week after I found the test, that I really had to come to terms with the lingering question in the back of my mind. All night, I lay awake waiting for her to get home from work. When she did, she hesitated in the hallway much like she did weeks before. Then she turned and went into her old bedroom.

When I woke up Monday morning, I peeked into the room. She was curled up in a tight ball on the bed, gripping the blankets in front of her so tightly it almost looked like she was awake. My heart broke when I saw that. It was a painful, miserable sort of confirmation.

For some of that week, I forced myself to consider that she wasn't pregnant at all. Maybe she didn't actually have anything to tell me. She could have suspected that she was pregnant just because of how she was feeling and the fact that we hadn't been particularly careful, took the test, and found out it was negative.

But the later the week progressed, the more I realized that didn't make any sense. She was acting so strange, and if she wasn't pregnant, she would have no reason to hide the test and not tell me about them. I would expect her to tell me she had taken a test as soon as she saw me again.

Which left me with only one thing to think about. Only one realization I had to come to terms with. If she didn't want to tell me she was pregnant, it was because she could be pregnant with Marshall's child rather than mine. Just the idea of that was eating me up. I couldn't stand the idea of her carrying that guy's baby. It infuriated me and made me feel sick.

Not that it would mean that she had done anything wrong. They were together for a long time, and I couldn't just pretend nothing ever happened in their relationship. It hurt so much because everything—everything about our relationship, everything about what we could have into our future—was completely different now.

She didn't want to tell me, so she was leaving me completely in the dark, and I hated that. I hated the idea that she was hiding something so huge from me and didn't trust what my reaction might be to the situation.

That might have been the worst part about it. If it was Marshall's baby, did that mean she wasn't intending on staying? Maybe that's what it was. She knew she was pregnant with his child and intended on going back to him, telling him about the pregnancy and seeing if they could work things out.

Not that I saw that going particularly well for her.

Marshall wasn't known for his compassion and I didn't doubt that he would shirk responsibility for anything that interfered with his plans for himself.

I wanted nothing more than for her to be happy. I had done everything to try to give her a chance to be happy here. And she couldn't even have enough respect for me to tell me the truth and let me know what was going on.

Without bothering to pack her a lunch like usual or even leave her a note, I slammed the door and headed out to work. It didn't even matter to me if I woke her up. Right then, I just wanted to be away from her.

The anger carried me through the rest of the morning and past lunch. The rest of the team sat around the field together, enjoying the picnic the Freeman family set out for us, but I sat off to the side and ate sullenly by myself. As soon as I was finished, I stormed back to the garage and buried myself in work.

It didn't take long for Quentin to come corner me. I didn't want to talk to anyone, let along my boss. I just wanted to be by myself and work until I forgot my problems. But he wasn't going to give me that option.

"Greg, what the hell is going on with you today? I get that you're still going through a lot with your dad dying and trying to figure everything out, but the last week, you've been really off. Did something happen?" he asked. "Is there something any of us could do to help you?"

I wanted to push him away. I wanted to just get in his face and tell him it wasn't any of his business, that he needed to back off and leave me alone. But that was just my fury. It was my frustration and anger talking. Quentin didn't do anything wrong. None of this was his fault, and all he was trying to do was be a friend and extend support and encouragement to me.

And right then, I couldn't just throw that away. I needed to let it out, to release the pressure and strain, and to have someone else give me their perspective.

"I'm sorry. There's just a lot going on."

"Come on," he said. "Let's take a walk."

"We just got back in from lunch," I said.

"Good thing I'm the boss then," he said. "There's some donuts in the breakroom. I noticed you didn't have any dessert with your lunch. Let's go fix that."

He brought me to the breakroom behind the garage, and we sat down with glasses of juice and donuts. He let me nibble at it for a few moments before he gave a leading nod toward me.

I sighed, wondering where to begin. Finally, I just dove in.

"It's Maya. Everything has been going really, really well between us," I said. "Like, better than I ever could have imagined it could have gone. But then a little more than a week ago, she said she wasn't feeling well and that it was the takeout we ordered. I was really worried about her, but she seemed to have it totally under control, so I didn't press her about it."

Quentin nodded, a knowing look on his face. "I think I might know where this is going."

"It was the weekend of the race when we stayed out of town. I wanted her to just be able to relax, so she stayed home and rested. Then when I got home, I expected her to be up, but she was asleep. I went into the bathroom to take a shower and accidentally kicked over the trash can. There were a bunch of pregnancy tests at the bottom. Totally hidden."

"Were they positive?" Quentin asked.

"The results weren't readable anymore. They had been

sitting around too long. So, I decided I was just going to let her bring it up when she was ready. I figured if they were negative, she would tell me she took the test and was still feeling sick, so she was going to go to the doctor. And if they were positive, I figured she would tell me that, too," I said.

"And?"

"And she hasn't said anything. Nothing at all. I've been doing my best not to push her, but she just keeps pulling further and further away, and I just can't believe she hasn't said anything. So, then it occurred to me that the baby might not be mine."

"What do you mean?" Quentin asked.

"Maybe she is pregnant but is far enough along that she knows it's Marshall's and not mine. And she is just hanging around until she figures out what she's going to do. And what if that's going back to Marshall? I just don't know what to do."

I looked at Quentin, waiting for him to come up with a brilliant response for me. He was one of the most level-headed men I knew, and he didn't disappoint. He didn't even have to think.

"I know exactly what you should do," he said.

"What?" I asked.

"Talk to her."

"Talk to her?"

"Yes, talk to her. Don't guess. Don't assume. You don't actually know what's going on at all, and you're letting yourself get all worked up and upset over something that might not even be real. You need to talk to her," he said.

I thought about that for a few minutes and tried to come up with a reason to argue against his point, but I knew deep down that he was right. I needed to just grow some balls and talk to her.

"I will," I said. "Thanks."

As easy as it was to say that I would talk to her, I knew actually doing it was going to be much more difficult. In all honesty, I didn't know if I could handle the truth if my suspicions were right.

31

MAYA

Like Sunday, Thursday had taken on a new, strange feeling. Before now, Greg and I both looked forward to Thursday all week. We knew that was an evening we would get to spend together. I was really enjoying my job, especially now that I was helping out more with the cooking, but I was always eager to spend more time with Greg.

At least that's the way it used to be. Thursday I woke up not sure if I even wanted to be at the house when he got home. I didn't know what to think about what was going on between us. It wasn't unusual for us to not see each other much during the week. That had been the way it was since I started working for Lindsey.

It was essentially the same routine, just in reverse, a constant rotation. The only times when that was broken up were Sundays and Thursdays. And occasionally on Saturdays if he didn't go up to the complex to finish things up before I went to work.

So the fact that I hadn't spent any time with Greg in days in and of itself wasn't all that strange. It was actually to be expected. And yet, it felt uncomfortable and uneasy. It was like just one more reminder that something wasn't right between us.

We had fallen out of the habit of leaving each other food, and we didn't even text during the day. There were even moments when things happened or I thought of something and wanted to share them with Greg, but I stopped myself because I didn't know how he would think or react if he heard from me. It was easier to just not say anything to him than to reach out and have him ignore me.

All that morning I pattered around the house just trying to fill time. I cleaned and did laundry. I tried to do a little bit of baking but couldn't find the heart. At lunch, I sat in front of the TV and watched mindless old shows while I ate.

By the middle of the afternoon, the sadness was really getting to me, and I knew I needed to do something to shake myself out of it. I didn't want to get in the car and go anywhere, but I needed to get out of the apartment.

I changed into my bathing suit, checking myself in the mirror to see if anything had changed about me. I was still very early in my pregnancy, so I couldn't really expect to have a pronounced bump. But it looked like there might have been a little bit of new softness there. Just a very slight difference that meant in the weeks to come this baby was going to let itself be known.

I was going to have to come up with some way to either tell Greg or to finally come to terms with having to walk away. As I walked toward the pool, I hoped nobody was there. Especially those guys who'd shown up the night I was there with Greg. They were obnoxious and rude, and I just didn't have the patience to deal with them.

Fortunately, I saw the entire pool deck was empty. In a strange twist that seemed a little bit like the universe was taunting me, my apartment complex resident card showed up in the mail early in the week. It meant the landlord had added me to the lease, and now I had a card to access the pool and the mailbox.

It was like right when things should look like they were falling into place and becoming permanent, that was exactly when it was all falling apart.

I walked through the gate and chose the chair that was in the fullest sunlight. Draping my towel across it, I sat down and put my sunglasses on. Letting out a sigh, I rested back and let the sun wash over me. Its warmth was reassuring and comforting, and I felt myself finally relaxing.

The afternoon started to slip by as I lay there, and soon I felt hunger starting to rumble in my stomach. I had learned what that meant. Not just that I would be hungry and very quickly move to ravenous if I didn't heed the call, but that it was very likely I would start to feel sick as well.

It was something I'd learned both from listening to my own body and from reading the papers the doctor had given me. Apparently, keeping a little bit of food in your stomach at all times helped to keep blood sugar levels stable and ward off pregnancy sickness.

I was starting to reluctantly sit up and pull off my sunglasses when I heard something so unexpected I barely even knew how to process it.

"Maya?" a whimpering, tear-filled voice called from a distance.

It was a voice I knew very well. But one I never would have expected to hear in Charlotte, much less in my apartment complex. I sat up straight and pulled off my sunglasses, my head snapping over to the gate leading to the pool. Ashley stood there with her hands wrapped around the bars of the gate, her forehead resting on them as she stared through at me. Even from this far away, I could see how red and swollen her face was.

I got up and walked toward her, opening up the gate so she could come through.

"Ashley? What the hell?" I asked.

She looked horrible. She was pale and thin, and I couldn't help but notice dark bruises stretching from her shoulder to her wrist on one arm. She stumbled a few steps toward me, shaking her head.

"He... he... I couldn't let him," she stammered.

I put one hand on her back and gently guided her over to the chair where I was sitting. She sat down on it. Despite the anger, betrayal, and disgust I had felt for my former friend, I couldn't help but be worried at how awful she looked and sounded.

"Tell me what's going on," I said.

"I couldn't let him hurt my baby."

I was stunned at her words as she broke out into sobs, and I reached out to gather her up in my arms and hold her tight to me. She shook and trembled, her sobbing hard enough to rock her entire body. I held her that way until she calmed enough to stand again.

"Come on with me," I said. "We're going to go to my apartment." Wrapping my arm tight around her shoulders, I helped her to her feet. "Are you okay? You feel like you can walk?"

"Yes," she said, nodding.

"Good. Let's go."

We walked slowly back to the apartment. I unlocked the door and let her inside. I brought her right over to the couch and sat her down.

"I'm so sorry," she managed to get out.

"You don't need to apologize right now. I'm going to go

make you some tea, then we're going to talk about what's going on. Just relax."

I went into the kitchen and filled the kettle with water. Setting it on the stove, I reached into the pocket of the jogging pants I had thrown on over my bathing suit. I took out my phone and quickly sent a text to Greg. If there had been anybody else I could have contacted at that moment, I would have. But I didn't have an option. I needed help, and he was the most reliable.

It was quick and to the point, simply asking him to bring home pain medicine safe for a pregnant woman. I was fairly certain that was going to lead to a whole conversation we needed to have anyway. But I couldn't think about that right then.

I'd never seen Ashley like this. Even when we were at our closest, I'd never seen her this upset, this clearly devastated and afraid. I was extremely worried about her, especially her mention of a baby.

It made my stomach turn to think of Marshall doing something to her that would put her in this condition. He'd never laid a violent hand on me, but I knew that he had a temper.

Being pregnant myself only made it more difficult, and I could put myself in her shoes. I knew how vulnerable she was already feeling, how scared and unsure of her future she might be. To add being terrified of the man you lived with and who was supposed to love you sounded horrifying.

The water finished heating, and I poured it into cups with my favorite tea bags dangling over the side. I let them sit for a little while as I filled a tray with honey, milk, sugar, and cookies. When I went back out into the living room and sat down beside her, Ashley was curled up, her knees to her chest as she rocked back and forth.

"Drink this," I said, handing her one of the cups of tea. "Do you want anything in it?"

She shook her head. "No, this is fine. Thank you. I'm so sorry to just show up here. I know you must hate me, but I didn't know where else to go."

I shook my head. "Don't worry about that right now."

I mixed a little bit of milk and some honey into my tea and breathed in its wonderful smell. I took a couple of sips, then reached for a cookie. As much as I wanted to know what had happened and what brought her all the way out here to Charlotte to find me, I could tell she just needed a few moments to regroup.

She drank her tea and nibbled her way through a cookie. It looked like she was just about to start talking, and I reached over to take her hand. Suddenly the door to the apartment burst open and Greg rushed in. Ashley jumped, letting out a high-pitched gasp like she was afraid of who it might be.

Greg stopped short just in front of the couch. "Fuck."

He lifted his hand up from his side, holding out a pharmacy bag. I took it, and he sat down in the chair across from us. I couldn't look him in the eye. Not yet. But I would eventually. Once I knew what was going on and was able to help Ashley, I could figure out what was going to happen next for Greg and me.

"You got here fast," I said, still not looking at Greg but pouring some of the painkillers into my hand.

"I left as soon as I got your text," he said.

I nodded and held the pills out to Ashley. "Take these. Don't worry, they're safe for the baby. They'll make you feel better."

"Thank you," she said.

She tipped the pills into her mouth and swallowed them with a gulp of tea. I reached over and rubbed her back.

"Just relax," I said. "Do you need anything else?"

"No," she said.

She looked exhausted, but I didn't push her. She needed to be able to decide what she was going to do and when. It looked like she hadn't been allowed to make a choice like that in a long time.

GREG

If there was even the slightest bit of lingering question about my feelings toward Maya, that one text message from her took that all away. When I first heard my phone alert me to a message, I didn't think much of it. My mother and I had been communicating more recently, though there were still a lot of things up in the air. It also could have been Darren, who wasn't at work that day, checking in.

When I saw Maya's name on the screen, I was surprised. She and I had been barely even acknowledged each other's existence for a few days. It just seemed like everything about our connection had fallen apart. There were no more lunches tucked in the refrigerator with sticky notes. No more dinners to come back to when she was at the bar.

We didn't text each other, and she was sleeping in the spare room every night rather than coming into bed with me. Taking Quentin's advice when he first gave it to me seemed so easy. After all, it was logical. Just talk to her. There was something serious going on, and I needed information, so I needed to get it straight from her.

But just as I thought, it wasn't as easy to actually do it as it was to acknowledge it was what needed to be done. I tried to come up with how I was going to start that conversation. It would need a careful introduction. Or not an introduction at all.

I was still in a place where I wasn't sure how to feel about the situation.

At least, I was right up until I read the text message from Maya. She needed me to bring her painkillers that were safe for a pregnant woman. Right there, the hammer came down. Not only was she pregnant, but there was something wrong. She needed medicine, and whatever was going on was serious enough that she didn't want to leave the house, or couldn't leave the house, to get it on her own.

There was no way I was going to make her wait. I needed to talk to her. I needed to be there with her and make sure she was okay. My heart started pounding so hard in my chest I could feel it in my throat, and my head felt a little woozy.

I shoved my phone in my pocket and gathered everything up, cleaning my station just enough that my tools wouldn't be a danger to anybody else in the garage. As I headed out, I looked over at Gus.

"I've got to go," I said. "I'm really sorry to be dipping out like this, but I need get home. It's an emergency. I'll let you know what's going on when I get a chance."

Before even giving him the opportunity to answer, I rushed out and ran to the parking lot. That was one of the mornings when I took my bike to work, and I pushed it to its absolute limit to the pharmacy. I didn't know what medications were safe for a pregnant woman and a developing baby.

With that in mind, I went straight for the pharmacist to

ask for his recommendation. He looked at me with widened eyes, obviously startled by my intensity. He clearly thought I was on the edge. To his credit, he stayed calm, gave me the information I needed, then got out of my way.

I bought what he pointed out to me along with a bottle of ginger ale and raced back to the apartment. Horrible images were going through my head by the time I got there. Maybe she'd hurt herself. Maybe she was sick. Maybe something happened to the baby.

But I never would have expected to run into the apartment and find Ashley sitting there on the couch beside Maya. The only reason I recognized her was because of the picture Maya showed me on Marshall's social media the day the two of them moved in together. This was the girl who had been one of Maya's close friends.

She was also the girl who Marshall had apparently cheated on Maya with. But now there she was, sitting on the couch in our living room, her face streaked with tears and looking beaten to hell.

As soon as Ashley took the painkillers I brought, I went into the kitchen to make myself some of the tea the girls were drinking. It smelled good, and at that moment, it sounded like it would probably do me good. While I was in there, I sent a text message to Gus. I didn't want him worrying about me.

I also knew he would immediately think about Maya, and I didn't want him worrying about her, either. I didn't know if Quentin had told his father what was going on. I hadn't specifically asked him not to, but he hadn't said anything to me about it. I reassured him everything was fine with me, and with Maya, and asked him to let everybody know.

His response came almost instantly, like he had been

holding his phone waiting for me to message him. He said he was glad that everything was okay and to keep him in the loop. He wanted to be there to help if there was anything he could do.

When my tea was ready, I went back into the living room and sat down. Ashley was already in the middle of a conversation with Maya, but I was able to catch the last few words.

"It was horrible," she said." I had no idea he was going to react like that. I mean, we never talked about having children. It wasn't something that ever came up in a conversation. We never really talked about anything."

"I thought the two of you were pretty serious," Maya said. "You moved in together right after I left."

Ashley nodded again. "I thought so, too. He really made me feel like I was the most important thing in the world. That he couldn't wait until it could be just the two of us and we were going to have this amazing life together. But then this happened. And I didn't even know what to do. Never in a million years would I have thought Marshall would do something like this."

"I would have," I said.

Maya shot daggers at me with her eyes. "Not now Greg."

"Hi, Greg. It's been a while," Ashley said. "I'm sorry to show up like this without calling or anything."

"Look, the reality is, Marshall is a jerk. He always has been," I said. "It shocked me to hell when I found out that Maya had been in a relationship with him for as long as she was. Back in the day, I knew him to have a short temper and a massive attitude problem. He could be violent and impulsive. I never heard specifically about him hurting anyone, but it's not something I would immediately put past him."

Ashley shook her head and dropped her face down into her hands. "I really thought he was going to kill me. I thought he was just going to toss me off the balcony or smash my head into the wall. It was the most terrifying experience of my life."

"Right," I said, setting my tea down and looking at Maya. "So, can I kill him *now*?"

I had held back for far too long. I needed to get it out. I wanted to go to Shelby and throttle the bastard. What he did to Maya was enough. This just pushed everything over the edge. But Maya wasn't on board with that plan.

"No," she said. "No, you can't. That wouldn't help her at all. It wouldn't do any good, either. And, frankly, I just don't have it in me to deal with having to go all the way back there just to bail your ass out of jail."

"I have nothing," Ashley said. Her voice sounded as though she had just come to that realization. "I really don't. I actually told my mother about the baby first. It would be her first grandchild, and I thought she was going to be excited. That was so stupid of me."

"She was upset?" Maya asked.

"She was beyond furious," Ashley said. "She was so mad that I was telling her I was pregnant but not married. Right then and there, she told me to leave and not come back. She didn't want anything to do with me anymore. I can't go home. I have nowhere to go. No job. Nothing. I know it was ridiculous to come here and find you, but it was the only thing I could think of."

"It wasn't ridiculous," Maya said. "We were friends once. And if you needed to escape, Charlotte's a good place to escape to. Trust me, I know."

Ashley managed a weak smile. "Marshall found out you were here in Charlotte. He was talking about it every day for a while, like he just couldn't believe you actually made it without him. It almost felt like he was hoping you were going to come crawling back to him."

"No," Maya said. "I don't think that's it. But I do think he absolutely wanted me to fail. He didn't want to think for a second that I could somehow be okay in life without him there to pull me along."

"I just don't know what I'm going to do," Ashley said. "I needed somebody to talk to, and I just kind of ended up here. But now, I have no idea what I'm supposed to do next."

Maya looked at me. Our eyes locked on each other over the sobbing woman, and I nodded.

"You don't need to worry," Maya said. Ashley scoffed, but Maya leaned so she could look into her face. "Listen to me. You don't need to worry. Everything is going to be just fine. We are going to figure this out one little bit at a time. And that starts with you knowing you absolutely have some-where to go. Right here. We have a spare room, and you are more than welcome to crash in it."

"I can't put you out like that," Ashley said. "Not after what I did to you, Maya."

"You won't be putting us out," I said.

"And it's not forever," Maya added. "I'm going to call Lindsey. She showed me an apartment behind the bar."

"I'll do it," I said. "You stay with Ashley. Help her get cleaned up."

I went into the other room and called Lindsey to ask about the apartment. She seemed confused but said it was available. I told her I had a tenant for her and that I would get it set up. She agreed, still sounding befuddled, and I hung up. That night was about making sure Ashley was okay, and then we would focus on actually getting her settled into the apartment.

More than just helping Ashley, that night was about reconnecting with Maya and finding out what was going on. I couldn't stay away from her anymore. I couldn't deny my feelings and pretend I didn't love her with everything I had.

33

MAYA

I went into the bedroom and grabbed a pair of stretchy pants and a T-shirt. Bringing them back into the living room, I reached out for Ashley's hand. I helped her to her feet and brought her into my bathroom.

"Here," I said, "take a shower. It'll make you feel so much better. Here's some fresh clothes for you. There's all sorts of body wash and exfoliators, everything you can think of. I went a little bit crazy when I found the body products shop in town. And when you're done, let me know. I'm going to put fresh sheets on the bed in the spare room so you can get some rest. Are you hungry?"

"No," she said. "I'm fine, really. This is all too much. You're being way too nice."

"I'm not being too nice," I told her. "It's like you've forgotten how close we used to be."

"I just can't believe you're being so kind after what I did to you," she said.

I shook my head as I put the clothes down on the counter in the bathroom. "You didn't do anything to me. Marshall did. He's the one who cheated on me, not you.

Maybe your discretion wasn't the best, but we both know how manipulative he is. Just like you said, he makes you feel like you're the most important thing in the entire world. Like it's the two of you against everybody and everything else. Nobody can deny that."

"I just wish it hadn't been you," Ashley said. "You were one of my best friends. And I managed to let him wiggle his way in and ruin all of that. I let him manipulate me into throwing all of that away. I just hate that I was that easily swayed."

"It's not like you're the only one. Besides, I don't want to talk about him anymore. It's not about him. This is about you and your baby. I want to make sure that you're okay. What he put you through is unforgivable. There's no excuse for him to put his hands on you. Trust me, I know how scary it is to suddenly not know what you're supposed to do because your life has just completely gone up in flames."

"At least you ended up here and much better off," she said. "Greg is amazing."

"You ended up here, too," I said. "And we're going to make sure that everything works out just fine for you. Hear me?"

"Yeah," she said. "Thank you. So much."

I smiled at her and started the shower. "Relax and enjoy. One of the fun perks about this apartment complex is that water is included." I winked at her, and she laughed. "I'll be right outside if you need me. You can just call."

I stepped out into the hallway and closed the door behind me. As soon as I turned around, Greg was right behind me. I gasped and pressed my hand to the middle of my chest.

"Sorry," he said. "I didn't mean to startle you."

"It's okay," I said. "I'm just a little bit on edge. It's been kind of a rough evening."

"That's for sure," he said. "Can you come into the bedroom with me? I think we need to talk."

I swallowed hard but nodded. I knew we needed to have this conversation. I just wasn't completely prepared to have it right then. I was still freaking out about Ashley, and I hadn't come to a total conclusion about how I was going to handle this talk with Greg. But the time had come, and there was no more putting it off.

I took a deep breath and followed him into the bedroom. He mimicked my breath as we sat down on the bed, and he looked into my eyes. "I'm glad you messaged me today."

"I'm sorry if I upset you. And that you had to leave work. I didn't realize you were going to come that fast," I said.

"There was no way I was going to let you sit around and wait if you were hurting or sick. I just had no idea it was for somebody else." He hesitated for a second. "I also thought you were telling me you were pregnant."

And there it was. The big old elephant in the room he didn't even know was there but had suddenly made its presence known. There was no turning back from this now. I drew in another breath, holding it in my lungs for a few seconds to try to make myself stop shaking.

"I am," I said.

Greg looked at me with shock in his eyes, like he didn't know how to respond. He had gone from thinking I was pregnant to thinking I wasn't, and now he was back to the confirmation that I was. It was a lot to process within a short period of time.

"Is it Marshall's?" he asked.

That question hit me hard in the chest. It felt like he had reached through my rib cage and was squeezing my heart. Never for an instant did I consider that he might think that. It made me want to cry. I couldn't even imagine how much it would hurt him to think that. Or how horrible it would be if that was the reality. That made my heart reach out to Ashley even more.

I shook my head. "No. It's yours. I've known for a couple of weeks. I just... it was such a shock. When I found out, I couldn't really wrap my head all the way around it, and I didn't know how you were going to react. I needed to figure out how to tell you, but then things got weird between us. You are pulling away, and I didn't want to make it more complicated by telling you."

Greg looked at me strangely. "I was pulling away? That's what you think?"

"Yes," I said. "When you came back from that race, you were different. It's like you didn't want to talk to me. You've been strange and distant ever since then. I thought that you had just changed your mind about us, and I was going to have to deal with that."

"I was strange when I came back from that race because I was waiting for you to tell me you were pregnant," Greg said.

I blinked at him a few times, trying to process what he just said. "I don't understand."

"When I got home from that night, you were asleep. I was really worried about you because you had been feeling so poorly for so long. I didn't want to wake you up. So, I went to take a shower, and I was trying to be careful, but I ended up kicking the trash can."

"And you found a pregnancy test," I said with a sigh, closing my eyes and cringing.

Greg nodded. "A whole bag of them. I had no idea what to think. It was so overwhelming standing in there and looking at all these tests, not having any idea what they meant."

"And it had been too long since I'd taken them for the results to still be present. So, you wouldn't have even known what they said."

"I didn't," Greg said. "All I knew is that you had taken a bunch of pregnancy tests. Which, to me, meant you thought you were pregnant. I didn't want to say anything to you because I wanted to give you the chance to bring it up to me when it was right for you. And then you didn't. And then you didn't. And then you still didn't. And it really started to get to me."

"Why?" I asked.

"Because I had to wonder why you weren't telling me. I figured it had to be something bad, and that you were pulling away from our relationship by not telling me. It was killing me, but I didn't know what to do. I just kept waiting, but I started worrying that maybe it was Marshall's baby and that's why you hadn't said anything about it."

I wanted to kick myself. All of this confusion and misunderstandings just because neither one of us had opened up to the other one. I collapsed against him, relieved as hell and just ready to let everything go and put this behind us. I wanted to move forward. He gathered me up into his arms and held me close.

"I'm so sorry I didn't say anything to you," I said. "I was just afraid. We've never actually had a conversation about what our relationship is. We just kind of fell into it and I was dumb enough to be insecure about it and wonder if we were on the same page. And I couldn't face telling you I was pregnant and having you only want me to stay because of a baby."

"I would never do that," he said.

"In my heart, I know that," I said. "You're not that kind of guy. And before you keep feeling guilty, I can completely understand why you would be upset thinking I was pregnant with Marshall's baby."

"It wasn't exactly the most pleasant thought," he admitted with a short laugh.

"I'm sorry for all of this," I told him.

He shook his head and a lopsided grin formed on his handsome face. "Me too. And by the way, I'm super excited for this baby."

"Me too." I jumped into his arms for another hug. We pulled back and looked into each other's eyes for a second before he kissed me.

I let out a long breath when our mouths parted. "What are we going to do about Ashley?"

"I feel so bad for her going through all this," Greg said. "She looks terrified. And those bruises are bad. Unfortunately, I can tell you that if we can see those, there are a whole lot more we can't see. She needs some help right now."

"I'm so glad to hear you say that," I said. "As soon as I saw her, my heart broke for her. I hate that Marshall cheated on me with her. But I would have hated that he cheated on me with anybody. The fact that it was my closest female friend was horrible, but I know how manipulative he is. Beyond that, it doesn't matter who you are or what you've done, nobody deserves to be treated the way he treated her. I'm determined to make this better for her. I can't just leave her hurt like that."

"No, you can't," Greg said. "Neither of us can. Tomorrow, we'll talk to Lindsey again and figure out how to start getting Ashley on her feet again. You know, maybe this is..."

"This is what?" I asked.

"Maybe this is why I came into that money. It came to me for a reason. With that, we can make sure Ashley is well taken care of until she can figure everything out on her own and take care of our family, too. It's all going to be okay," he said.

In that moment, I completely and utterly fell in love with him. I had always loved Greg, but it felt different now. I was completely consumed with my love for him, and I couldn't imagine spending another moment of my life without him.

34

GREG

Now that we were on the same page about helping Ashley and about our own relationship, all I wanted to think about was my baby. For that brief amount of time when I thought it was possible she could be pregnant with our child, it was both exciting and terrifying. Being a father wasn't anything I'd ever thought about, but now that I had absolute confirmation that my little one was growing inside her, I couldn't *stop* thinking about it.

Suddenly, the idea of having a child with Maya was the most natural thing in the world. I had only known about this baby for a few minutes, but already it was real and precious. Never again could I imagine life without my little one.

Wrapping one arm around Maya's waist, I rested the other hand on her belly and stroked it with my thumb.

"Tell me everything," I said. "Have you gone to the doctor? What do you know?"

She giggled and pressed her hand over mine. "I don't know a lot. It's still really early. But, yes, I did go to the doctor. I missed you so much while I was there."

"I wish I could have been there," I said. "What did you

find out? Does everything look okay?"

"So far, everything looks really good. There isn't a whole lot the doctor can tell or see right now because it's so early, but apparently everything looks good and she has me scheduled for my next appointment in a couple of weeks," Maya said.

"I will definitely be at that one," I said. "And every one after that."

"You don't have to do that," she said with a laugh. "They aren't always exciting. It's not like there's going to be an ultrasound every appointment or anything. But you can come to as many of them as you want."

"Deal. When do we get to know if it's a boy or a girl?"

She laughed again and shook her head in. "It'll be a while before that. And I'll do a blood test to find out, or we could wait another couple of months after that and find out with an ultrasound. But I'm not sure I want to know."

I looked at her with wide eyes. "What do you mean you don't know if you want to know?"

"Don't look so shocked. I just don't want to know ahead of time, that's all. I think it would be fun to have the old-fashioned moment in the delivery room when right after the baby's born, the doctor announces it's a boy or it's a girl. Doesn't that sound like fun?" Maya asked.

"That doesn't sound like fun. That sounds like months and months of waiting for something we don't have to wait for. It's considered old-fashioned for a reason. We have the technology, Maya. We can know."

"What is the big deal about knowing ahead of time?"

"That way we can think about how to decorate the nursery and names. I just feel like if we know as soon as possible, we can start really connecting with the baby," I said.

"I'm connected to the baby without knowing what it is," Maya said. "And besides, doesn't surprise sound wonderful? There are so few real surprises in life. Why would we want to throw one away?"

I did my best not to growl with exasperation and frustration. "I hate that excuse so much," I told her. "Yes, finding out what the baby is when it's born is a surprise. But so is finding out what it is before. You're still just as surprised when you find out what the baby is through a blood test or an ultrasound. Aren't you?"

She seemed to think about that for a few seconds. "You know, I never saw it that way."

"Perfect," I said. "Then we'll find out as soon as we can."

She shook her head and leaned over to give me a kiss. Across the hall, the sound of the shower went quiet, and a few minutes later we heard the door open and close.

"I'm going to go check on her," Maya said. "I'll be right back."

I closed the door behind her and changed into my pajamas. It felt good to slip into my side of the bed and leave hers open knowing it would soon be filled. She wasn't gone long before slipping back into the room with an armful of clothes.

"How is she doing?" I asked.

"About as well as she could be, I think," she said. "We are having a pretty good giggle over being pregnant at the same time. But she's exhausted, and I think she just needs to rest."

"I'll call Lindsey back in the morning, and we'll get everything squared away," I told her.

She changed into her pajamas and slid in beside me, resting her head on my chest like she always did.

"Thank you," she said.

Within moments, she was asleep.

Like almost always, I woke up before Maya the next morning. I slid out of bed carefully and was almost to the door when I remembered Ashley was in the apartment. I couldn't just wander out there in pajama pants and nothing else. I changed into my clothes for the day and went out into the living room. It was still quiet. Apparently, Ashley was still asleep as well.

The first call I made was to Gus.

"I was getting worried about you," he said as soon as he answered.

"Everything's fine," I said. "Things just got kind of thrown up in the air really fast, and I had to get them all figured out before I could let you know." I gave him a basic rundown of what happened, not wanting to get too far into detail because it would drag the conversation on long and I had other things I needed to do. I was sure we would talk again soon. "Can I take the day off today?"

"The team doesn't have another race until next week, so as long as you're ready for that, we're good. You do what you need to do," Gus said.

"I will be ready, I promise," I said.

"I'm sure you will. I trust you. You know I have quite a few connections in this town, and in other places, too. If you need me in any way, don't hesitate. You know where to find me. I will do anything I can for you."

My heart felt warm, and I smiled even though he couldn't see me. "Thank you. For everything. For always being there for me."

"Of course. I always will be. We're family," Gus said.

When I got off the phone with Gus, I called Lindsey. She sounded just as worried and confused as Gus did. Possibly even more considering she told me Maya was convinced I was going to break up with her, so when I called the day before and said I had somebody to move into her apartment, she thought it was her.

"I was just about to kill you," Lindsey said. "I mean, I would have done it nicely and swiftly considering your link to Vince and the rest of his family. But definitely killing you all the same. I thought you had a lot of damn nerve calling me to arrange for Maya to come live in my apartment because you wanted to get rid of her."

"Well, that's definitely not the case," I said. "Did she tell you anything else?"

She paused briefly. "What do you mean?"

"Is there anything else that she told you? When she told you she thought I was going to break up with her, is there any other news she happened to share with you?" I asked.

"No," she said. "She didn't say anything but that you two were drifting apart and you were being weird, so she thought you were going to break up with her. Why? What else is going on?"

"A lot, actually."

I gave her a more detailed explanation of everything that was happening than I gave Gus. Not just because Lindsey knew Maya better than Gus did, but also because she was a woman who had experience with pregnancy and struggling with an ex. It wasn't exactly the same thing as Ashley was going through, but it was enough to give her more empathy and compassion.

Lindsey was also, just in general, one of the kindest and most giving people I had ever known. I was hoping she would be able to help Ashley out, in more ways than just renting her the apartment. Ashley needed as many friends as she could get right now, especially those who could identify with what she was going through.

She sat in what seemed like stunned silence for several seconds after I stopped talking.

"Lindsey?" I asked. "Are you there? Did you hear everything?"

"I definitely heard everything," she said. "I'm trying really hard not to totally bubble over with reaction right now. I cannot believe Maya is pregnant, and I am so excited for the two of you I can't even stand it. But we're going to put that aside right now because we need to talk about Ashley. She sounds like the one who really needs help right now."

"She really does. She's a complete mess. And Maya is being absolutely incredible about her. I doubt I've met many people in my life who would be so open and willing to not only accept the woman their partner cheated with, but to go completely out of their way to help her."

"That's just the kind of woman Maya is," Lindsey said. "You've got a good one."

"Don't I know it," I said. "And I always have. Do you think you can help?"

"Absolutely," she said. "No way I'm going to leave somebody out in the cold after going through that. She can definitely move into the apartment behind the bar. I'll give her the first month with no rent so she can get on her feet. As for a job, I can help her out with that, too. If she's interested, I just lost a server. I offered it to Maya, but she wasn't into it. She's really enjoying cooking. Ashley's welcome to that."

"Thank you so much, Lindsey. You are making a world of difference."

Feeling like things were falling into place and everything was really going to be okay, I went to the kitchen to start making breakfast. I felt like I was hedging in on Maya's territory a little, but I wanted to spoil her some. I was feeling guilty for all those days of missed lunches, but I also just wanted to make sure she was feeling taken care of.

By the time the ladies woke up, the table was full of food, and I had just finished brewing a fresh pot of decaf coffee. I welcomed them to sit down and filled their plates. Then sat down with them.

"Okay, Ashley, this is how it is. The first thing we are going to do is call the police," I said.

Her eyes widened, and she shook her head. "No. I can't do that. There's no way I could go talk to the police and tell them everything. Marshall would be so angry, and I would be so embarrassed."

"There is no reason for you to be embarrassed," Maya said. "No reason at all. You didn't do anything wrong. Marshall can't get to you. It doesn't matter if he's angry. I will go with you to talk to the police. You don't have to be alone."

"No, you don't," I said. "I'm not going to let Marshall get away with this. And neither one of us, or any of our friends and family here in Charlotte, are going to let you fend for yourself. Coming here was the best thing you could have done. First of all, you have an apartment now. Lindsey is not only willing to let you stay in it, but she said she won't even charge you rent for the first month so you can get on your feet."

"And I've seen it," Maya said. "It is absolutely adorable. You'll love it. And I work at the bar, so I can easily come and check on you, and we can hang out."

"Well, you can hang out at Ashley's apartment," I said. "Or you can hang out at work."

"What do you mean?" Ashley asked.

"Lindsey has a job for you too. If you want it, she has a server position you can start immediately. Or whenever you're ready," I said.

Tears welled up in Ashley's eyes. She hung her head and cried into her coffee, but after a few seconds she agreed. After breakfast, we called Nick Freeman.

"Hey," I said. "Can you ask Gabe if his friend Clint is working today?"

"Sure," Nick said. "Why? What's going on?"

"Maya and I have a friend here who needs some assistance from the police," I said. "And I thought it would make her feel better if she was talking to somebody we were familiar with."

"Sure thing," he said. "I'll have Gabe call him. And if he's available, should I send him over to your apartment?"

"Yes, please," I said. "How is everything with you? Bryn doing okay?"

"Doing great," he said.

"Good to hear. Hopefully I'll see you guys sometime soon."

"Absolutely," Nick said. "We'll be at the family barbeque Sunday."

An hour later, Gabe's police officer friend, Clint, showed up at my door. Maya and I sat with Ashley the whole time she talked to him, encouraging her to tell him everything and not hold back any details. He took the report and suggested she contact a lawyer just in case. After he left, I texted Darren to get the name of the company lawyer. We were going to make sure she had everything she needed.

35

MAYA

Everything felt right in the world by falling asleep in Greg's arms again. I felt comfortable and safe curled up in the nook of his arm and shoulder, my head rested on his chest so I could hear his heartbeat. I was so happy and finally feeling like life was smoothing out and settling into place.

But as soon as that thought went through my head, I went back to thinking about Ashley and what she was going through. I knew that situation was far from over. Gabe's friend Clint was so kind coming over and talking to her about what happened. He was willing to take down the report and record all of the information and details she would give him.

He also made sure she understood that the assault had happened outside of his jurisdiction. Since the incident happened in Shelby and not in Charlotte, he couldn't go and arrest Marshall. All he could do was make sure the information was on file here in Charlotte in case anything else happened while Ashley was here and encourage Ashely to report Marshall to the Shelby PD.

Before we could deal with any of that, though, we needed to help Ashley settle into this new phase of her life. She admitted she really didn't have a plan when she left Shelby and ended up driving to Charlotte to see me.

I nestled closer to Greg and propped my chin on my hands to look into his face.

"Something on your mind?" he asked.

"I want to make sure she's okay here," I said. "And I know we've already made sure she has somewhere to live and gotten her a job, but that's not everything. When I left, I at least got a chance to prepare. Marshall gave me a day to gather all my things and leave. She left in a total panic because it was an emergency. She didn't get a chance to bring anything with her."

"He can't keep her belongings," Greg said. "Just because she was living in his apartment doesn't mean he now owns everything that's hers. She absolutely has the right to go back and get her things. But I don't like the idea of her going back there by herself."

"I don't like the idea of her going back there at all," I said. "After what she went through, she shouldn't have to face him. And I know I didn't want to go anywhere near Shelby when I first came here. Did you want to go back after you left?"

"Not at all," he said. "I don't even want to go back now. But I'm going to."

I lifted my head and looked at him. "You are?"

"Of course I am. Like you just said, she shouldn't be going back there. Not right now, anyway. She shouldn't have to face off against Marshall. It's better if she's just here and we can give her a chance to decompress."

"What are you going to do?" I asked.

"Tomorrow, I'm going to call a couple of the guys, and

we are going to go down to Shelby. He won't start anything with a bunch of guys he doesn't know and me. And if he does, he's going to regret it quickly," Greg said.

I settled down into his chest again, but for only a second before popping back up. "You're not going to beat him up, are you?"

"Not if he doesn't ask for it," he said.

"Let's make sure he doesn't ask for it."

He didn't answer, and I decided to just accept that and settle in for sleep. The next morning, I woke up with him so I could make him breakfast before the guys came over. I fully intended on sleeping for another couple of hours before going to work, but I didn't want to miss an opportunity to kiss him goodbye.

And to remind him not to cause any trouble.

Greg was still working his way through a towering platter of orange rolls and coffee when Darren and Colby showed up. They knocked on the door, and I let them in. As soon as they walked in, they were drawn to the smell of the rolls, and soon all three men were sitting around the table eating and conspiring for the day.

They were hunched over the table, their heads close together as they talked about how they were going to go into the apartment and how they would handle any number of different situations. It was almost like listening to little boys playing spy. If it wasn't such a serious situation, it would almost be adorable.

When they were finished eating, Greg took the key from Ashley along with a list she had made of everything she really wanted from the apartment.

"Are you sure you don't want me to go with you?" she asked. "You shouldn't have to do this by yourself."

"I am absolutely sure," Greg said.

"So am I," I said. "You need to stay here with me and just let them handle this. Marshall decided he wanted to play dirty, so now it's time for you to play your hand."

Greg came up to me and gathered me into a hug, then gave me a kiss.

"Don't kill Marshall," I said. "Okay? I kind of need you here to help raise this baby."

He leaned down and gave me another kiss.

"I'll do my best," he said.

The guys waved at me as they headed out, and I looked out the front window to watch them climb into Darren and Greg's trucks to head on their way. As much as I hated the idea of them going into a situation that could be uncomfortable or even dangerous, they seemed to relish it. It made me feel warm, and love bubbled up in my chest. He was a good man. I was so lucky to have him.

I started toward the bedroom to lie back down, promising myself I would do the dishes when I woke up.

"I'm going to grab a couple more hours of sleep," I said to Ashley. "Make yourself at home. If you want to go down to the pool, I put my resident card on the side table for you."

She thanked me, and I headed into the bedroom to crawl under the sheets. They still smelled like Greg, and I smiled as my eyes closed and I sank into sleep.

When I woke up, I headed into the kitchen to get something to eat. I hadn't eaten anything before the guys came because my stomach was feeling sensitive that morning. When I walked into the kitchen, Ashley was standing at the stove scrambling a couple of eggs.

"I hope you don't mind," she said. "Scrambled eggs are just about the only thing I'm able to eat in the morning without feeling sick."

"Of course I don't mind," I said. "I told you to make

yourself at home. I know all about having to eat what your stomach says you can."

She gestured toward the frying pan with her spatula. "Do you want me to scramble you up some, too?" she asked. "They're really gentle on your stomach because they have so much protein in them, and it helps you feel more stable throughout the day, if that makes sense."

"That actually sounds really good, thanks," I said. "I have to head into work in a couple of hours, and it would be really nice to have some energy and not worry about feeling sick."

Just as I said that, my phone alerted me to a new message. I figured it might be Greg updating me on their mission, but instead, it was Lindsey.

"Is that the guys?" Ashley asked.

"No," I said. "Actually, it's my boss. Our boss. Apparently, I don't have to go into work today."

"Is everything okay?" she asked, tipping the fresh eggs onto a plate and setting them aside so she could start another batch.

"Everything's fine," I said. "She just got a last-minute booking to rent out the bar tonight. That happens sometimes. It started a couple of months ago, apparently. Somebody asked if they could have their anniversary party at the bar because that's where they had their first date. She was kind of reluctant to do it at first, but then she did, and people really love it."

"It's surprising that she would close down the bar on a Saturday. Isn't that her busiest day?" Ashley asked.

"Yeah, usually," I said. "But she's been taking last-minute bookings more and more recently. Honestly, she's not all that concerned about losing money by closing on a busy night. She would rather have the customers be happy."

"That's nice of her," Ashley said, sounding slightly suspicious.

I laughed.

"It's not as magnanimous as it sounds. You'll find out that Lindsey is one of the nicest people on the face of the planet, but the reason she's so willing to take time off and close down the bar so that people can rent it out is because she is marrying a multimillionaire. Multi-multimillionaire. Some whispering around here says he could be a billionaire. But nobody really knows for sure."

"How does nobody know for sure?"

"He just doesn't talk about it. He's one of the Freeman brothers. That's the family Greg works for at the racing company. They are all extremely wealthy, but you wouldn't know it by hanging out with them."

We carried the eggs and a fresh pot of decaf coffee over to the table.

We sat and ate, gradually rediscovering the friendship that had fallen by the wayside. I didn't want to mention any of the awkwardness, but it seemed there was something heavy weighing on her mind.

"I need to tell you something," she said.

That didn't sound good. Very rarely do conversations that start with that phrase ever go well for the person on the other end.

"Go ahead," I said.

"I didn't want to tell you this at first, because I thought it might sound like I was just making excuses or was lying to make things better. But I really want you to know. Marshall and I didn't sleep together until after you two broke up."

I looked at her strangely. "By the way you were talking, it sounded like the two of you were embroiled in some huge, dramatic love affair."

"That's the thing," she said. "That's how he wanted me to look at it. He made all these big gestures and talked about us like we were the epic reincarnation of all the great relationships throughout history. But I wouldn't have sex with him knowing that he was still with you. I think it was all a game to him. He liked knowing he could control my emotions so much. And he enjoyed the chase. He was trying really hard to convince me to sleep with him. But I just wouldn't. I think that's why he asked you to move out so suddenly."

"Asked me is kind of a gentle way to put that, but that does make sense. If he got tired of waiting for you, he would do whatever he needed to in order to convince you to give him what he wanted. He is manipulative as hell."

"So, you believe me?" she asked.

"I do," I said. "I'm sorry he put you through that and hurt you the way he did."

She gave me half a smile. "I am, too," she said. "You didn't deserve what he did to you either. He should have been honest with you. Actually, I should have been honest with you. I should have told you from the beginning what was going on and let you make the decision, not him."

"Not your responsibility," I said. "That was his job. But you know what? We don't have to worry about him anymore. Greg is picking up your life and bringing it here, and you are starting over. You and your little one are going to be just fine."

3 6

GREG

The mission to go get all of Ashley's stuff from Marshall's house in Shelby was surprisingly anticlimactic. The guys and I were all pumped up for a showdown if it had to happen, but it didn't.

The most dramatic part of the whole experience was just being back in Shelby. I hadn't been in my hometown since the day I left it five years ago, and it was almost like traveling through time. As soon as we drove into town, I was right back to my high school years. Absolutely nothing had changed. It looked exactly the same as I remembered it, which was both reassuring and a little unnerving.

It almost felt like if I stay there too long, I would get sucked right back into it and never leave. When we got to Marshall's place, he wasn't there. We knocked on the door several times and attempted to look through the peephole, but it seemed empty. I used Ashley's key to unlock the apartment door, and we went in armed with a couple of boxes, duffle bags, and the list of what she wanted.

The entire time I was in there, I was braced for Marshall to show up. I wondered if he would recognize me.

236

If he didn't, I would make sure he remembered me. It was petty and possibly a little childish, but I wanted him to look in my face and know the boy he'd talked down to and treated like trash had grown up to be not only a more powerful and influential man than he was, but also independently wealthy.

I also wanted him to know Maya was in *my* bed now and carrying *my* child. He had lost everything.

But he never showed up, and we were able to gather everything and get out in a relatively short time. When we got back to my apartment, I found Maya and Ashley cooking together in the kitchen. I stood quietly and watched them for a few moments. It was good to see her at peace alongside the woman who had contributed to so much pain.

In all honesty, it didn't matter to me so much if they rekindled their friendship and became as close as they used to be. I wanted to make sure Ashley was alright and help her get a new start in life. In the end, what mattered to me the most was Maya's happiness. Being able to put that conflict behind her would do her good.

Not able to stay away from her any longer, I went into the kitchen and wrapped my arms around her waist, leaning down to kiss the side of her neck. She giggled and curled into the kiss, reaching up to put her hand on the back of my head. She turned over her shoulder and kissed me.

"I didn't even hear you come in," she said.

"That's because the two of you were talking so much," I said with a tease in my voice. "Something smells good in here. What are you making?"

"Ashley's famous fajitas," Maya said. "She even taught me how to make fresh guacamole."

"Sounds amazing," I said. "When's it going to be ready?"

"Just a few minutes," Ashley said. "We're just finishing up the vegetables and warming the tortillas."

"Perfect," I said. "I'm starving. But that'll give the guys and me time to bring everything in."

Leaving them to finish up dinner, I went back outside and Darren, Colby, and I took three trips to bring in everything. We had even managed to snag a couple pieces of furniture Ashley told us she had moved into the apartment and wanted back. It left Marshall's place looking pretty picked over, but he deserved the shock when he got home.

We all sat down to dinner, and Ashley thanked us for going on the recovery mission for her.

"Not a problem," I told her. "Oh, I almost forgot. It's a very good thing we went and got all of your stuff today."

"Why?" she asked with a questioning expression in her eyes.

"Because I got a call from Lindsey when we were on the way back from Shelby, and she let me know that the apartment is ready for you to move into tomorrow."

Ashley's face lit up, and she jumped into my arms for a tight hug. The mood for the rest of the evening was celebratory, and we all went to bed happy.

Monday morning dawned bright with Ashley no longer in the spare room, everything of hers transferred over into the apartment, and Maya naked in my bed. I liked that last bit the most. Lying there for the first few blissful moments of the day was wonderful. I was beyond glad that we had finally gotten our shit together and worked everything out.

We were good and we were settled. The drama was mostly over, and it felt like life was just waiting for us. But that meant now we really needed to get serious and talk about our baby and what we were going to do about our future. The first thing that came to mind when it came to that topic was my apartment.

When I'd picked this place out, it was fully intended to be a bachelor pad. That's all I was at the time, and I didn't see any point in the near future, if at all, when I would be anything else. It definitely wasn't the type of place I wanted to raise a child. Now I had the means of finding a real home, and I wanted to talk to Maya about that as soon as possible.

She was still asleep when I left for work. I stopped at the doorway to the bedroom just to look back at her for a few seconds. It was so good to have that rhythm back. Right down to leaving lunch for her in the refrigerator. The sticky note told her that I would be coming by the bar for dinner later, so she didn't need to make anything. But again, I would always accept dessert.

The thing that Minnie Freeman did not make that Gus absolutely loved was donuts. I stopped by my favorite donut shop on the way into work and grabbed a huge assorted box. I also got a couple of bags of Gus's absolute weakness: gourmet vanilla coffee. Topping my order off were two cups of fresh brew. When I headed to the complex, my first stop was Gus's office.

Technically, since he was retired, he shouldn't have an office anymore. But he never really moved out and just ended up hanging around. He still stopped at the office every morning to check emails and read the news before heading down to the garage. That morning I caught him right as he seemed to be getting up to make his way down there.

He looked surprised when he saw me but invited me in. I sat down and offered him one of the cups of coffee I was carefully balancing on top of the box of donuts. He took it and smiled happily as he breathed in the sweet vanilla smell wafting up from the cup. I sat down with the box on the desk in front of me.

"I wanted to come by this morning and thank you for being so amazing to me," I said. "I know things have been a little crazy recently and you could have just sent me on my way."

"No, I couldn't have," he said. "That's Quentin's job. Quentin could have sent you on your way."

His face was absolutely straight for a few seconds, and then he grinned, his eyes sparkling as he started to laugh. "There's no way we would let go of you," he said. "Greg, you're family. We would do anything we could to take care of you. And that includes Maya."

"That actually brings me to the next thing I wanted to talk to you about," I said.

He took a sip of the coffee and looked at me curiously. "Oh?"

I didn't want to tell him everything, as Maya and I hadn't decided how to tell people about the baby yet. So far, Lindsey knew, along with Ashley, but I didn't want to just start spreading it around without her being involved. So, I just skipped over that detail.

"I want some real estate advice. Now that I've come into this money, it doesn't make as much sense for me to just stay in that apartment anymore. Especially with Maya here. I think I'm ready to buy a house and really put down roots."

"That's fantastic," Gus said. "Congratulations."

"Thank you. I just have no idea where to start," I said.

"I'm happy to help you however I can," Gus said.

By the end of the day, I had a stack of listings Gus had found for us along with the contact information for a real-tor. I headed right for the bar with the three listings I had narrowed the options down to. Maya was already out of the kitchen, standing behind the bar with Lindsey when I walked in.

She smiled when she saw me and stood up on her toes to lean over the bar and kiss me.

"How was your day?" she asked.

"It was really good," I said. "I have something to show you."

"Okay. What is that?"

I handed her the papers for the three listings. She took them and looked over them. Her eyes slid back up to me, and one eyebrow lifted. There was something about that look. I couldn't really put my finger on it, but that simple little quirked eyebrow combined with her crisp white chef's jacket seriously got to me. My jeans got a little tighter, and I had to fight to control myself.

This woman was definitely it for me. I never thought anybody would be able to affect me so much, and she did it effortlessly with just the simplest of moves.

"Houses?" she asked. "This is what you wanted to show me?"

"Yeah," I said. "I asked Gus for some advice about good realtors, and he gave me the contact information for one. He found these listings for us, and they had everything I told him I was looking for."

"And that is?"

It was almost as if she was so hopeful, she didn't want to really accept what I was saying for fear of disappointment. I was going to need to be up-front and straightforward with her so she could understand I was building our future.

"The apartment was good for me. It was even good for us. But maybe it's not so great for when the baby makes three," I said. Her eyes locked onto mine, and I saw Lindsey go completely still beside her.

"Are we talking about this now?" Lindsey asked cautiously, keeping her voice low.

Maya met my eyes again, tilting her head just slightly toward me to ask me to make the decision. I nodded.

"Yeah, we're talking about this," Maya said.

Lindsey let out a shout of excitement and threw her arms around Maya. All I could do was laugh.

3 7

MAYA

Lindsey held me tightly and jumped up and down as she laughed and cheered. I looked over her shoulder at Greg and rolled my eyes at him. He shrugged, trying to look innocent. I couldn't believe he just blurted it out like that. It wasn't like nobody in the world knew. Ashley knew, and I had a feeling Greg had told somebody. But we hadn't talked about making an announcement yet. I was still very early on in my pregnancy and hadn't decided yet how or when to tell everybody in my life.

It was not so much something for me to think about anymore. From the way Lindsey reacted, it occurred to me that Greg had already told her. I didn't know when or why, but he had spilled the news already. She had done admirably well not telling everybody in creation. But now that it was out in the open, the news was fair game.

That was why it didn't surprise me in the least when she immediately whipped out her phone to call Vince. While she talked to him, I leaned against the bar toward Greg. He tried to avoid my stare but finally looked at me.

"So, when did you tell Lindsey?" I asked.

"Um," he said, "maybe when I called to talk about Ashley and the apartment?"

The tone in his voice was funny, and I laughed, shaking my head. "Can't keep a secret at all, can you? I managed to keep it in for two whole weeks."

I gave him a mischievous smile, and he grinned back, nodding.

"Making fun of yourself and the misunderstanding that nearly ended our relationship. Nice."

"Too soon?" I asked.

Greg shook his head. "Not at all. You are ridiculous, and I love you."

He pushed down on the bar to lean over and kiss me.

I had to go back into the kitchen to work, but it seemed like only a few moments later when Lindsey called me out to the bar again. I walked out and saw what seemed like the entire Freeman crew gathered around Greg.

The boys were all patting him on the shoulder and giving him slap-on-the-back-hugs while the women were smiling and whispering to each other. They all cheered as soon as they saw me. I laughed, getting that overwhelmed feeling again that I got the first time I spent time with them. But it was still a good feeling.

I walked out from behind the bar and immediately into a cloud of hugs and kisses on my cheek. They were coming at me so fast and continuously I could barely process who I was interacting with at any given point. All I knew was I heard women's voices telling me they were so excited to talk to me all about my pregnancy and for our babies to grow up together and the men telling me how happy they were to have me part of the family. When I got to Minnie, she held me close in a warm, maternal hug that brought tears to my eyes.

"Welcome to the family, honey," she murmured. As I stepped away from her, she slipped an envelope into my hand. I didn't have the time to open it right at that moment, and she didn't seem to care whether I did. I slipped it into my pocket, wanting to look at it when I was alone.

I tried to make my way through the crowd to get to Greg, but by the time I got to the stool where he had been sitting just moments before when I was standing behind the bar, it was empty. I looked around, and Lindsey leaned toward me.

"Darren and Colby snagged him for a game of pool," she said. "If it's like any of the epic showdowns they usually have, it'll probably be a while."

I laughed. "Well, they've already met her, so it's not a big deal. But I think this would be the perfect opportunity for everybody to meet Ashley."

"That's a great idea," Lindsey said. "Why don't you go get her from the kitchen?"

I went into the kitchen and found Ashley scraping plates into the trash can to hand to the dishwasher. She was already working extremely hard and was very popular among the customers. I could tell she was going to do really well here.

The best part about it, though, was that she looked happy. She seemed to be enjoying the atmosphere and the job itself. It would be months before her pregnancy progressed to a point where she would have to stop working, and I was confident Lindsey would make sure there was something available for her when that time came.

It was good to see her having fun and feeling good about herself while she worked. She looked up at me and smiled when I came into the kitchen.

"Hey," she said. "What's all that commotion going on out there?"

"Actually, that's why I came in here," I said. "Why don't you come out there with me?"

She looked at me strangely. "Why? Is there a table who needs me?"

"Not exactly," I said. "Come on. I have some people I want you to meet."

She set the dishes down and wiped her hands, nodding. She had only been in town for a little while, but she was already looking healthier and stronger. She was wearing long sleeves to cover up the bruises, but they were starting to fade, and soon she would have no more trace of Marshall's violence visible.

All that would be left as a reminder of him would be the baby. While that was a monumental reminder, we had already talked about it. Ashley had already stopped thinking of the baby as being a part of Marshall. It was just hers, and that was all that mattered.

I brought her out front and introduced her to everybody. They welcomed her with warmth and acceptance just like they had for me. I could see how much it meant to her as her smile grew wider and a faint sheen of happy tears came to her eyes.

When she was done meeting everybody, we went back into the kitchen together. She wiped her cheeks and turned to hug me.

"Thank you," she said. "I can't tell you how much it means to me to have you introduce me to your family. And to have them accept me like that."

My heart swelled at her description of them as my family. I loved that she could see the bond so strongly already.

"They are amazing people," I said. "And completely genuine. None of that was fake or put on as a show to be polite. That's how they actually are. But I do have to warn you about something."

Ashley braced herself like she was getting ready for terrible news. "What?"

"Now that they've met you and welcomed you into the fold, you're going to be expected to come to all the activities and events. That includes family dinners and picnics at the compound," I said. "You might even have to come to a race."

She grinned, her shoulders relaxing as she realized that was the warning. "I think I can deal with that. It might be a struggle, but if I have to face hanging out with awesome people and eating really good food, it's just a sacrifice I'm going to have to make."

I wrapped my arm around her shoulders and gave her a squeeze. "I knew you'd fit in around here."

The crowd at the bar started to pick, so both of us had to concentrate on work again. The next couple of hours went by quickly. I'd thought being in the scrub position was hard work but switching over to cooking was a completely different animal.

The shift in challenges and responsibilities was a lot, but I had an absolute blast doing it. It made time go by quickly, and by the end of the night, I was, as always, completely exhausted, but surprised my shift was already over.

That night, the end came even sooner than I expected. The Freeman family and everyone who had come along with them stayed well into the night, and when the last of them, including Greg, decided it was time to leave, Lindsey came over to me and nodded toward the door.

"Get out of here," she said.

"What?" I asked.

"Go on home," she said. "Get some rest. Remember we talked about you having new hours now. Well, that starts tonight. Clock out and go home."

I hugged her and rushed to clock out. When I got back out front, Greg greeted me with a hug and a kiss. We walked out to the parking lot, and I saw he had brought his bike.

"Give me a ride home?" I asked.

"Seriously?"

"Have you forgotten the bikes you used to build when we were kids?" I asked. "You always gave me rides on them. I miss that."

"Are you sure that's safe for the baby?" he asked.

I nodded. "As long as I'm not doing it when I'm eight months pregnant, yes. This one time won't hurt either of us."

He finally relented, and I climbed onto the back of his bike with him. As we rode home, I thought about how much my life had changed. Lindsey bringing up the shift in my hours reminded me just how far I had come. The bar was transitioning over to having a full lunch service and dinner service followed by a late-night menu that went into action at ten each night, switching over to simple finger foods.

This meant rather than working the latest hours, I would be working at the end of the lunch shift and into the dinner shift. Being able to leave at ten at the very latest meant I would get home in time to see Greg every night. It mirrored how I felt I was changing and growing in life. Coming up from the bottom and building the life I wanted. The life that felt so incredible to have finally achieved.

Being wrapped around him and feeling the strength of the machine beneath me revved me up. By the time we got home, I only had one thing on my mind. I completely forgot about the envelope in my pocket in my rush to tackle Greg and drag him off into the bedroom with me. Just the thought of being able to do this every night was enough to make me almost insatiable.

38

GREG

Morning came earlier on Tuesday than it usually did. There was a race that evening, and it was a long haul, so we had to leave early. I told Maya she didn't have to get up with me, but she said she wanted some time with me before I would be gone for another couple of days.

I hated that idea, but I felt like it was a good thing that we were getting used to it now. Neither one of us had the energy to make a huge breakfast like we usually had, so we settled for warming up some of the baked goods she had made a couple of days earlier and stored in the freezer. She was sipping a cup of her decaf coffee when her eyes suddenly widened.

"What's wrong?" I asked. "Did something happen?"

"No," she said. "It's okay. I just remembered that Minnie gave me that envelope last night."

"What envelope?"

"When you went off with the guys, I was talking to everybody. I got to her and she gave me a big hug, welcomed me to the family, and handed me an envelope. I had no idea what it was, so I just put it in my pocket. It felt weird opening it in front of everybody else."

Maya wiggled a little bit like an uncomfortable feeling was going down her spine. "I put it in my pocket and completely forgot about it. I wonder what it is."

"Why don't you get it? We can open up before I leave for the race if you want to."

She nodded and rushed off into the bedroom. A few seconds later, she came back with a plain envelope in her hands. It looked fairly thick like there were several documents in it. She sat back down and flipped the envelope over in her hands a couple of times. Larger than a standard-sized envelope, it didn't appear to have any logos or indication of what might be inside.

"It doesn't say anything on it," she said.

Slipping her finger under the edge of the seal, Maya inched the envelope open. Once it was open, she reached her fingers in and pulled out the first folded stack of papers. She unfolded them, and I watched her eyes scan over the documents before she handed them over to me.

"What is it?" I asked.

"Insurance information," she said. "They put me on your policy."

"Oh, good," I said. "I'd ask them to do that."

"You did?" she asked. "When?"

"When you were feeling so sick and worried about going to the doctor. You mentioned you didn't have any insurance. At the time, I had no idea what was going on. But I wanted to make sure you could get the medical care you need at any point, for any reason. So, I asked Minnie if she could figure out how to add you to my policy through them."

"I can't believe you did that," Maya said. "That's so sweet."

"I just want to take care of you," I said. "In any way that I can. And it might not be the most romantic gesture in the world, but I hated the idea of you not getting care or suffering needlessly just because you didn't want to go and face a high bill. Actually, now that I say it out loud, that is actually the least romantic gesture I could ever make for you."

"No, it's not," she said. "You're taking care of me. Us."

She ran her hand over her belly, and my heart warmed. I put my hand over hers, and we took just a moment to savor the feeling of being the three of us.

"What else is in there?" I asked a few seconds later.

She reached into the envelope again and pulled out another stack of papers. This time when she opened it, her mouth fell open and her eyes widened.

"I can't believe they did this," she said.

"Did what?" I asked. "What is it?"

She handed the papers to me. "It's stock papers. They gave us stocks for the baby."

Suddenly, her face crumbled, and she burst into tears. I wrapped my arms around her and held her while she cried. I was still trying to get used to the waves of emotion that came with her pregnancy, but I was willing to be there by her side through any of it.

I hated that I had to leave. I didn't want to be away from her, and I especially didn't want her to be alone when she was so emotional.

"Promise me you will keep in touch with Lindsey and Ashley until I get home," I said.

Maya pulled away from me and nodded, wiping tears from under her eyes. "I'm supposed to have dinner with them at the bar tonight. I guess it doesn't really count, since we'll all be working. But tomorrow, Ashley and I are going to get together before work to shop for a couple of things for her new apartment."

"That's good," I said. "I'll miss you so much."

"I'll miss you, too."

I had already used up all the time I had that morning, and I had to rush to get ready and leave. I kissed her at the door and promised to call her that night.

The race was nothing short of uneventful. My competitors were having a great run, and I didn't even end up in the top five. Darren placed third, which was incredibly low for him. It was still in the top three, and he handled it well, but there was definitely a dampened feeling over us as we rode back to the hotel from the track.

As I sat there in the bus contemplating the race, I started thinking about my future. Maybe with a baby coming I should think about retiring and moving toward a safer position with the company. I had already gotten severely hurt once racing. There was no guarantee it wouldn't happen again, and maybe the next time it would be worse.

I thought about Maya riding with me back to the apartment from the bar. She was clinging to me securely, and we weren't going all that fast, but I was terrified every second. I didn't tell her. She was so excited to ride with me again, and I didn't want to take that away from her. But the whole time, I was worried about what could happen to her and to the baby.

If I was thinking about that, I needed to be thinking about the risk I was putting on myself every time I got on a bike. Especially when I was racing. I resolved to talk to Maya about it when I called her to say good night from the hotel. If I was really serious about this, I needed to tell her and get her input about it. These were decisions we needed to be making together. And there were far more of them to make as well. Our future was coming fast, and we needed to figure out what it was going to look like.

Though I never had a chance. As soon as I heard her voice, my body reacted, and things turned hot fast.

"I thought about you all day," Maya said, and something in her tone suggested the thoughts were more than just missing me.

"I thought about you, too. Especially now that I am all alone in this hotel."

"Oh no," she said in an exaggerated mock empathy. "You don't have me there to warm up the bed for you."

"Well, to be fair, we warm up the bed together."

There was a giggle on the other end of the line, and I smiled.

"I was actually thinking about warming up the bed quite a lot at work," she said, a lilt in her voice. My cock twitched in the loose pajamas, and I ran my palm over it.

"Oh really," I said. "I thought you were more professional than that."

"I just couldn't help myself," she said, the smile evident in her voice. "My mind just kept wandering to how much I wanted to strip you down."

"That's interesting, because stripping you down is what is going through my mind right now."

There was a pause and a rustling on the other end of the line, and then when she spoke again, her voice was a conspiratorial whisper.

"I'm naked right now," she said. "I'm on my side of the bed, and I can just imagine you here beside me."

I closed my eyes and imagined her soft, gorgeous body

under our sheets, her fingers sliding between her thighs as she spoke to me. Quickly, I unbuttoned the single button on the crotch of my pajamas. I pulled my thick cock out and began to stroke it.

"Are you touching yourself?" I said.

"Yes," she said, her voice breathy. "Are you?"

"Yes. Now, tell me what you imagined us doing while you were at work."

"Well, it started with me not wearing panties and you bending me over the prep station," she began.

39

MAYA

Greg had told me he didn't know when he would be getting back home from the race on Wednesday night, so as soon as I got home from work, I took a shower to relax the tension in my shoulder muscles, then crawled into bed. I had every intention of reading a few chapters of the new book I had started. After all, it was still several hours before when I was used to going to sleep.

But my hard work and the baby growing in my belly had other plans for me. By the time I got through the first chapter, my eyes were heavy, and I was drifting off to sleep. I closed the book and put it aside, turned off the lights, and quickly drifted off into sleep.

Greg showed up at some point a little bit later. I barely felt the bed move when he slid in next to me. I was just awake enough to snuggle up to his side and sigh happily. It felt better knowing he was home. The next thing I was aware of was waking up with morning light slanting through the window and illuminating Greg's face.

He was sitting up in bed, staring down at me. The baby seemed to have started a furnace inside me, and I was always hot, so I went to bed wearing nothing. Greg's eyes were locked firmly on my naked stomach, and his expression was pensive and slightly strained. I was still tired and really should have gotten more sleep, but his expression was so serious I knew we needed to talk.

I got out of bed and freshened up a bit, put on some clothes, and climbed back in beside him. He had thrown on some cotton lounge pants and a shirt. As much as I liked to look at him with as little clothes on as possible, this situation felt like it warranted clothing.

"I think you already know we have a lot to talk about," he said.

"Yes. We definitely do. What do you want to start with?"

He looked around, like he was taking in the entire apartment. "How about this place?"

"You know how much I love this apartment," I said. "But I think a lot of that comes from you taking care of me when I was so broken. As much as I don't want to leave those memories, I think you're right. This isn't the right place to raise a baby."

"It's not," he said. "And I want something that's ours. Like you just said, this apartment is mine. I picked it out, and I decorated it. I chose its features for what works for me. I want us to find a place that's perfect for us together, and for our little family."

"So, we're moving," I said.

He nodded. "Sounds like it."

"Wow. That's so grown-up."

He laughed. "It is. Now, how about you?"

"What do you mean?" I asked.

"You don't really need to work at the bar anymore," he

said. "I have more than enough money to take care of us. If you want to stop working, you can."

I immediately shook my head. "No. I'm not quitting. Especially not now that I finally got a job I love. Maybe that'll change sometime in the future, especially after the baby's born, but for now, I'm staying exactly where I am."

"That sounds fine," Greg said. "But what if I don't want to stay where I am?"

I narrowed my eyes at him. "What do you mean?"

"After the race last night, I got to thinking about my future. About our future. I think maybe it's time for me to consider retiring. Or at least limiting my races. I don't want to even think about getting hurt or worse now that we have a baby coming. I'm thinking about talking to Gus and Quentin and seeing if there's another place for me on the team," he said.

I was struck by that. "You would be willing to do that?"

"Absolutely. I would do anything for you and the baby. I don't want to take that much of a risk when I don't have to. What do you think?" he asked.

"It would definitely make me feel so much better if you weren't racing so much. I worry about you every single time you get out on the track. If there was another position for you, and you would be happy doing it, I think that would be the best choice."

"Speaking of choices," he said, and I laughed at his transitions. "What about us getting married?"

My eyes widened. "Are you proposing? Like this?"

"No," he said. "I'm not proposing. I'm just asking how you feel about it."

"Honestly? I don't want to get married just yet. I'm as surprised by that as you are by the look on your face, but I just don't feel the need for us to rush. You are my future, Greg. I have absolutely no doubt about that. So, I don't think we need to hurry through anything. I'm really happy with where we are right now, and I want to enjoy every stage of our relationship. How do you feel about that?" I asked.

"I know without a doubt that you're the only woman for me. I will spend the rest of my life with you. And we will get there whenever we get there," Greg said.

That brought a smile to my lips and a tingle to my stomach.

"So, why don't I show you just how good of a place we're in before you have to go to work?"

His fingers had been tracing up and down my lower chest and upper stomach while we talked, and I reached over, taking his hand and placing it on my breast. I slipped the shirt off and wiggled out of the pants quickly as he massaged it for a moment and my nipple hardened under his touch. I let out a breath as he dipped his head down to take my other breast into his mouth and swirl his tongue around the sensitive, taut nipple. My hips squirmed, and my core burned with anticipation as he slowly moved his kisses up my chest to meet with my lips.

Rolling over onto his back, he pulled me with him, and I laughed at the sudden weightlessness. When he was settled, I let my legs fall on either side of him and dipped down my head to kiss him again, this time our tongues sliding into each other's mouths for a taste. I felt his hands slide down my sides to my hips, and I rolled them in response. His thin pajama pants were the only thing separating him from my body, and I longed to take them off him. His hands made their way to my ass and squeezed tightly, and his cock twitched under me. It pressed against my clit through the silk pajamas, and I moaned, rubbing my core down the shaft.

With a slow rock backward, lingering as the head of his cock pressed at the pants to slide through my folds, I kissed down his chest and worked my way down his body. I let my lips press against his flesh, my tongue sliding out occasionally to run through the ridges of his muscles, until I reached his waistband. I glanced up to see him, his hands now clasped behind his head and a grin across his face. He wanted to enjoy watching me pleasure him, and the idea of his eyes on me, exalting me, craving more of me, spurned more heat between my thighs.

I slid my fingers under the waistband and pulled down gently. He lifted his hips so I could get them all the way off, and his cock sprung out. An involuntary moan rattled through my body at the sight of his glorious, thick cock, and before I even had his pants past his knees, I placed my lips at the head. My tongue swirled around it, and I watched him close his eyes and groan. I licked up the sweet, sticky fluid that had gathered at his tip and took him deeply into my mouth. Relaxing my throat, I took him as far down as I could manage, and his groans vibrated through his body and onto my tongue as I slid back up him, wetting him and stroking him in the process.

I twisted my hand as I reached the knob and went back down again, increasing the speed to suck him with passion. Little moans escaped my lips as I bobbed up and down on him, and I could feel his legs tense and repeatedly relax under my hanging breasts. Soon, one of his hands reached down to fill with my hair and guide me in a fluid, rhythmic motion. I closed my eyes and let the moment carry on for a while as my own other hand slid between my legs. As I touched myself, I felt the hand on my hair move away and trace down my back. It slid down between my ass cheeks and to my opening. As I swirled and applied gentle pressure to my clit, Greg slid a finger inside me, and I momentarily paused, his cock filling my mouth.

The overwhelming sensation of him inside me in both places short-circuited me for a moment, and when I began to bob again, it was vigorous and purposeful. His finger slid in and out of me, the pad rubbing along the upper wall. Tension built inside me, and I knew I wasn't going to last much longer before I had a climax that would make my previous short-circuit seem controlled. I groaned loudly as I stroked him, letting him slide out of my mouth while he turned me around and pulled me up over him, settling my core over his face.

His tongue slid through my folds, and I released my clit to let his mouth take control. He licked and pressed on my clit, and I took him into my mouth again, wanting to feel him inside me in every way I could. Suddenly, I felt like the pressure was too much, the need for release too great, and I slid down off his face to press the head of his cock at my opening. When I felt it in place, I sat down hard, and the tension inside me exploded.

I was facing away from him, and I leaned back to put my hands on his muscular chest. His hands wrapped around my waist and pulled me hard down on top of him. His massive cock filled me and stretched my walls. Then they molded around him, remaking themselves for him, and I rocked as wave after wave of climax washed over me. One hand slid up my side to clench my breast, and I leaned forward. Settling my hands on his shins, I rocked again and felt control seeping back to me.

His hands kneaded my ass, and I delighted in how much joy he took in the view. I bounced up and down on him, curling my head down to watch as well. He groaned as I rode him, and his grip helped me find a rhythm that was constant and full of explosive pleasure. I stayed there a while, enjoying the moment and the ecstasy of his cock filling me.

Suddenly he shifted under me, and I moved with him. I stayed on my knees as he sat up on his. One hand slid up my back and filled with my hair again. A slight tug made a wave of white-hot passion scream down my spine, as he took control. I was his, and I would pleasure him however he wanted. At that moment, it meant letting him fuck me from behind, asserting his control.

I closed my eyes and curled my head back as he slammed into me over and over, the pull of my hair enough to send that thrill through my core, but not enough to hurt. His other hand wrapped around me and a finger found my clit, swirling as he pulled me onto him. When his hand slid out of my hair, it went directly to my hip, and I knew he was close. The tension had been building again in me as well, and I knew the wave of another massive orgasm was coming.

Pushing my hips back into him and pressing my face down into the bed, I let my voice ring out with every thrust. There was no reason to hold back anymore, and I cried out with each plunge of his cock deep inside me. I heard his voice join mine in chorus, and then a deep roar drowned mine out. He exploded in me, and I shook as the mutual orgasm overtook me. He came hard and curled over me as he emptied himself, and then we both collapsed onto the bed, spent and happy.

I wished I could be standing beside Ashley, but she looked strong and confident. I was so proud of how she was handling herself. The courtroom was stark and unwelcoming, and the lawyer Marshall had chosen was like a bulldog, but she didn't back down. She didn't let them intimidate her or break her.

She stood there, brave and unyielding as she told them what he put her through. Her prominent, round belly was a powerful addition to her testimony. I watched her throughout the trial and noticed how she occasionally rested her hand against her belly, stroking it softly as if to comfort both herself and her unborn son.

Both of us were just about a month away from our due dates. We had gone through the entire pregnancy process together, and it had made us closer than ever before. Lindsey had even thrown us a joint baby shower just the weekend before. It was elaborate and completely over-the-top. Which, of course, meant it was absolutely perfect.

We were already joking that her son and my daughter

had no choice but to get married. We had already promised them to each other, and we would raise them to adore one another. That way we never had to worry about them dating somebody terrible. Greg was quick to point out that the fact that they would be born likely within days of each other and raised side by side meant they were more likely to be like brother and sister.

At that moment, I was only thinking about how proud I was of Ashley and the way she had managed herself throughout this entire experience. It wouldn't have been easy for anybody, but for a woman who was pregnant, it had to be even more of a challenge. And it was almost over.

Apparently, in more ways than one.

Ashley was just getting ready to speak when I felt a strange sensation and then a gush of fluid. I gasped, reaching over and grabbing onto Greg beside me. Ashley turned around to look at me.

"Are you okay?" she asked.

"My water just broke," I told her.

"What?" Greg asked. "But you're not due for another month."

"Tell your daughter that," I said. "Because she's on her way."

Ashley froze, staring at me like she didn't know what to do. Then she suddenly started laughing and turned to the judge.

"Your Honor, may I have a couple of moments, please?" she asked.

The judge was very understanding and waved her along. Ashley reached into her purse and pulled out her phone. She turned it on and called the EMT she had just started dating. At this point, the pain had started fast and intense. I described what I was feeling to Ashley when she asked, and she relayed the information to Brad.

"He wants to know if you feel like you could make it to the hospital on your own," she asked.

I was getting ready to say that I could, but another contraction hit me, and I doubled over.

"I'm going to go with a no on that one," Greg said.

Ashley told Brad what was happening and hung up. "He said they're on their way."

"I'll be fine," I said. "Just get me out to the car and bring me to the hospital."

"Absolutely not," Ashley said. "They'll get here and be able to tend to you on the way to the hospital rather than you having to wait until you get there."

I glanced over at Marshall and saw both him and his lawyer looking on in absolute horror. A few minutes later, the EMTs rushed in and helped me up onto a gurney. Marshall visibly recoiled, and Ashley leaned toward him.

"Don't worry, I won't call you when our son is born," she whispered loudly.

Part of what she was in court to settle was having Marshall sign away his parental rights. She said that was the part she was looking forward to the most. It wasn't vindictive or cruel. Marshall showed absolutely no interest in being there for his son and was eager to get rid of the responsibility. Ashley was just looking forward to being able to move on with her life without any ties to him.

She had finally gotten her spine back and I was so proud of her.

I couldn't help but laugh at the look on Marshall's face as Brad leaned over me on the gurney to kiss Ashley, and then they carried me off.

But the laughter didn't last long. Another wave of hard, intense contractions hit me by the time we got into the ambulance.

"We're not ready," Greg said. "The baby wasn't supposed to come for another month."

"I don't think we get a choice in this matter," I said. "She's decided today is her birthday, and there's nothing we can do about that. I'm sure the girls will help us get the nursery ready. We already have everything we need."

He nodded and took my hand, seeming to feel slightly more at ease.

The delivery was rough. It was happening too fast for me to even consider an epidural, and I felt totally out of control of my own body. At the same time, it was the most incredible experience of my life. And when it was over and I sat propped up in bed cradling her as she nursed, there was no question it was all worth it.

My daughter was less than two hours old when the room was invaded by a swarm of loud, excited people. All of the Freeman boys, their women and children, Colby, Greg's mom, Minnie and Gus, and even Ashley stuffed themselves into every space available to be there for her first visit.

It was wonderful watching each of them take their turn holding her and nuzzling her nose. Some of them tucked their faces down and whispered something to her. I wondered what they were saying, but I didn't ask. Those were her first secrets. They were hers to keep.

Greg sat on the edge of my bed, rubbing the back of my neck.

"I love you, you know?" he said, leaning down to kiss me.

"Well, that's good," I said. "Otherwise, all this would be really awkward."

We laughed, and I kissed him again before accepting Amelia back from Minnie. The older woman smiled at me and stroked my face softly. I might not have any blood relatives anymore, but this room was full of my family.

The End